Too Poor to Afford a Pencil

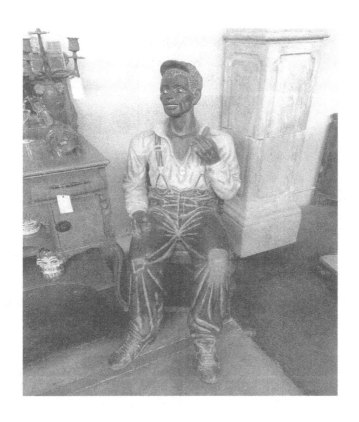

Samuel Ramos

NEWMAN SPRINGS PUBLISHING
320 Broad Street
Red Bank, NJ 07701

First originally published by Newman Springs Publishing 2020

ISBN 978-1-64801-600-4 (Paperback)
ISBN 978-1-64801-601-1 (Digital)

Printed in the United States of America

To Shirley and Rod

Reading on a Rainy Day

Reading on a Rainy Day

Reading has always been an essential part of your daily life. Something you started in grammar school and escalated and by the time you reached high school. Your choice of reading material in the beginning was above your comprehension. Gradually, you begin to understand the nuance of reading and took off from there. So, you embarked on a path of exploration. You started with *Origin of the Species* by Charles Darwin, then *On the Road* by Kerouac, *Howl* by Ginsberg, *The Poetry of Pablo Neruda* by Neruda, and *Tender Buttons* by Gertrude Stein. Your intelligence was no higher than the brightest kids in school, but your selection of books far exceeded what they were reading.

It wasn't just about reading a book. It had more to do with the written words. It was about how each author developed their characters and how they intertwined these characters in the plot of the story. Some books you could read in a day, while others would take longer simply because you looked for what wasn't written. Perhaps an underlying message.

Your interest in books helped formulate your creative side and spirit of adventure. In some stories, you lived vicariously through characters and felt a sorrow, pity, joy, depression because you lived how the characters lived. Engaging beyond just reading.

Your personal conversations or attachment to others drifted if they didn't read or weren't well read. How can you associate with someone who doesn't read, you think to yourself? And so, before graduating from high school, you were already a recluse or worse a snob, whatever side of the fence you came from.

As the years passed, your thirst for reading expanded boundaries that eventually began a manifestation of topics that neither affected nor distracted from your course of study. You read and studied Spinoza, the great philosopher with zeal. You began reading the entire work of Émile Zola, fascinated with his command of text. The works of Maxim Gorky, William Burroughs, and Ezra Pound...ever wondering how each could make the words they wrote dance with power. *Three Soldiers* by John Dos Passos, refabricating the lives of three soldiers during World War I, left you wondering about the need for war.

The readings didn't stop with the masters, you also read Bible, the Torah, the Koran, Confucius, Mencius, and Laozi. You found that God exist for all humans and not just a few as we tend to believe. For comfort, you took up reading mysteries and soon found that these writers wrote in such descriptive imagery, one couldn't keep from becoming one of their conflicted character.

You could read on a rainy day with comfort. You could read in the dead of winter under the covers, or read in the hottest day of the year while you sunbathed. You always had a book to read, and there was nothing as important, including being with the most beautiful woman imaginable or the best meal served with perfection.

If you learned anything about life, it came from Kerouac's *On the Road.* You came to understand life's conflicts with religion and witchery from the eyes of a child in *Bless Me, Ultima* by Rudolfo Anaya. Your studies of Taoism gave you an appreciation, an insight into the differences of life's transformations and how to accept each. This was your life changer.

If you find yourself deprived of all the lessons learned, then there is a good probability that tomorrow is undeserved unless you take up a good book. Hide in the closet until you come out dressed like the character you read about...that's the true meaning and lesson of reading.

People read and read and read, while you read to learn. To teach not preach and write about what is logged in your mind from all the millions of words you have come across, from the first day you opened a book.

Look into his eyes and see a world you have never appreciated before, the one that offers the most intriguing if not fascinating, sometimes glamorous view of life and beyond. He taught you how to look at life with a clearer view of where he has walked before and where he is headed. He has lived a million lifetimes, one word at a time.

Walk into the Light

Walk into the Light

"Should I lie face down in the gutter and drown in the mess that mankind has made? Me the humble man looking for salvation through others; while the wicked continue to be wicked!"

Ching Wa Li

Late in the evening, with the winds shaking the walls of my cabin, I sat in a dimly lit room with sadness and weariness pressed upon my chest. I knew that if I stop and listen closely, I could hear the sobs of my heart, longing for whatever my soul needs curing. I'm growing more sorrowful each day, and as a result of my internal turbulence, it's time for me to get up from this chair and search for whatever is missing in my life.

It's late September, and the winds from the northwest were gliding through the desert floor, picking up sand and dry desert brush, and slamming them against my face and body as I try hitchhiking from here to there. There's not a single car in sight. I can't even see beyond my thumb.

My only luxuries in life are the Levi's jeans I wear, two plaid shirts, a toothbrush, toothpaste, a pad and pencils, and a comb that I carry in my knapsack. I also have a Navajo woven blanket that I took off an old Navajo man whose frozen body I tripped over while ascending Mount Blanca, one of the four sacred mountains of the Navajo. Did I feel guilty for taking the blanket? No! If not me, then someone else.

My need to be with the indigenous people came one year earlier while walking through the San Carlos Apache Reservation where I saw sickly warriors working in fields that offered no hope of growing anything but despair. Their clapboard dwellings were no protection from the hot summer months or the howling winds and snow that crept through every crevice during winter. And the children in tattered clothes, with runny noses, sitting on old gas cans, looked for a handout from those who had nothing to hand out except a life of misery.

I sat with Delshay, the old Apache medicine man, in the middle of the darkest night of the month, drinking peyote from a canteen and talking about nothing in particular. Then, from time to time, the medicine man made growling sounds to frighten off the Coyote and the Owl.

In a slurred almost incomprehensible voice, the medicine man told me about the Coyote, the trickster, who occasionally was helpful to humans but oftentimes created havoc for everyone; and the Owl, who could take the shape of other animals and was used by the elders as the "bogeyman" to scare children.

I asked Delshay if he believed in God. He said nothing but then started to sing. He stopped singing and with searching eyes looked into my soul and said, "No earth, no sky, no sun, no moon. Only darkness everywhere. Then, a disc with one side yellow and the other side white appeared suspended in midair. Within the disc, a small bearded man, the Creator, the one who lives above and made everything." The old medicine man, drunk from too much peyote, got up and walked in his shack.

I continued sitting on the ground, my head spinning from the peyote, and I began writing in the dirt. I sat for another hour before walking into the darkest night of the month to reflect on what I had just learned.

The next morning, I awoke in a cave, stretched out next to a massive brown bear.

Frightened, I jumped and bolted from the cave. The big, brown bear called me back and said, "Don't be afraid. I won't hurt you." Hesitatingly, I returned to sit next to the stinking but kind bear. We talked until it was time for me to be on my way.

The brown bear provided food for my day's journey and a piece of hide with his paw print. Happy for the food but not understanding the paw print, I thanked the bear, and I set out to find truth or dishonesty, whichever came first. I walked for thirty miles through snake and scorpion-infested desert. I saw a cottontail rabbit being chased by the cunning fox while the hundred-degree heat continued beating down on my brain.

SAMUEL RAMOS

Without a drop of water to drink and only the food the bear had given me, my mind drifted from one subject to the next, and my body craved nothing; not even the companionship of the women I left behind.

Off in the distance, I caught sight of a man and a mule walking across the hundred-degree-plus desert. As I traversed more closely, I recognized him as my childhood buddy Jackie who had died twenty years earlier. "How are you?" I said, and with that ever-present smile he had so many years ago, Jackie said, "I'm doing fine," and continued walking with his mule. He stopped, turned around, and said, "See you soon." I wondered what he meant by that. I waved goodbye and resumed my journey.

I walked for ten more miles, my feet burning from the hot desert ground when I passed a gray-headed woman of sixty or seventy years of age, wearing a dark blue dress and white sneakers and who clung to an ornate walking stick that supported her unsteady legs. I inquired of her destination, and she told me her pilgrimage would end at a holy church that rested on a faraway mountaintop. I decided to keep her company. We walked in silence.

When we got to the base of the mountain, I was overwhelmed by the huge number of pilgrims walking up the range. I felt a spiritual connection with each and began praying for all my departed friends as well as for those still living. I climbed the steep, strenuous, and backbreaking mountain passage.

After two hours of climbing, I reached the mountaintop and saw a small church built from wood and rocks. I also saw a thousand pilgrims lined in single file waiting to enter the small church to offer prayers and ask for redemption for their sinful souls.

Scanning the site with my tired but curious eyes, I witnessed another thousand or more pilgrims sitting on the grounds surrounding the church, eating Indian tacos they bought from a little, old, gray-headed Indian woman and her barefooted grandson, who were having a hard time keeping up with the demand of the hungry pilgrims. Everyone ate in complete silence, but occasionally, you could hear the crunching of every delicious bite, including mine! After offering prayers to the heavens, I walked down the mountain encouraged that there was a God.

I continued walking, humming a song I remembered from childhood but couldn't recall the name. It didn't matter.

I came to the edge of the mesa, taking in the magnificent vista. I noticed a ghost town on the valley floor adjacent to a practically dry river. I trekked down the rugged mesa carefully watching where I planted each step, so as not to lose my footing.

As I made my way through a once prosperous little town, I observed cacti growing as high as houses; an old post office with the roof and two walls missing; a windmill and empty stockyard...railroad tracks that lead to nowhere; but mostly, what I saw were dilapidated wooden buildings ravished by wind, rain, and snow that shrieked through its main street and back alleys. In the entire town, only two buildings remained intact—a saloon with swinging doors and a church painted in brilliant white that stood at the end of the street.

I entered the saloon and stepped on loose wooden floorboards that creaked with my every step; I saw a weather-beaten wood bar with empty jugs of hooch on shelves, a huge ornate mirror on the wall and a spittoon.

I saw a gathering of old, gnarled men playing poker, smoking cigarettes and cigars, and drinking rotgut whiskey. Their loud voices overpowered the dance hall women who, in their worn, frilly, blue dresses and heavy makeup, danced to an unrecognizable tune being played on a piano with missing keys.

I sat on a rickety barroom stool of days long past and watched these men as they cheated one another and cursed the worst profanity imaginable while an old, mangy dog lay impervious to the ruckus around him. I was an apparition they never saw.

Afterward, I walked into the church with unadorned walls and half empty pews and found women and children singing hymns, while the preacher, dressed in black from head to toe, threatened and preached fire and brimstone from the pulpit. The organ player mended a pair of socks...and no one paid attention to anyone.

I wandered out of the town discouraged!

"Where are you headed?" I heard a voice from behind me ask. I turned around and saw a lovely, young woman with long brown hair and blue eyes, in a floral print sundress, sitting in a red Volkswagen. She asked me again, "Where are you headed?"

"I'm headed for the Pinal Mountains where I can rest and do some writing," I said.

"Hop in. I will take you." She smiled.

We drove all night, not speaking a word, just listening to rock 'n' roll music on the radio and stopping only once to buy gas, cheeseburgers, and coffee. I took the wheel, even though I didn't know how to drive. It made no difference; we were headed for the Pinal Mountains.

We reached the Pinal Mountains at midafternoon, tired and weary. I parked the red Volkswagen under a cluster of pine trees. I stretched my weary legs, while she stayed in the car and slept. I gathered pine needles with my hands, as best I could, into a mat and then covered the newly made layer with my Navajo blanket.

I then took out my pad and pencil, sat on the Navajo blanket, and commenced writing about the meaning of life as well as I understood it. I wrote well into the night and quit only when the darkness strained my eyes.

That evening, I gathered pine cones and twigs and made a roaring fire. I retrieved the half-eaten and cold cheeseburgers from the car, and we sat on the Navajo blanket and ate and talked, while the flames of red and gold from the fire danced into the sky.

As it turned out, her name was Gloria, a girl I once dated some years back. It was good talking and being with her again I felt safe. She stayed a week, and we survived on wild berries and love. Then, she had to move on. We made a promise to keep in touch, but it never happened. A month later, when I finally came off the mountain, I read that a drunk driver had plowed into the side of Gloria's red Volkswagen, killing her instantly. I saw my heart fall out of my frayed body…with my faith shaken, I would never be the same.

I stayed on the mountain for a month living on berries, wild onions, and mushrooms. I never feared the cold mountain nights or mountain predators. I didn't bother them, nor did they bother me.

One night, however, a pack of growling, hungry coyotes came to my camp; I could see their piercing eyes and razor-sharp teeth waiting for an opportunity to rip my body to shreds and have themselves a fine meal. I promptly reached in my pocket and pulled out the hide with the bear-paw and brandished it before the pack. They looked at each other with surprise before scurrying off, only to return later that evening with rabbits they had killed.

I cooked the rabbits on the open fire. We ate and talked about religion and politics and laughed and had a good time well into the next day. They continued to be my protectors during my remaining days and cold nights in the mountains.

With my protectors watching over me, I continued to write; however, the topics were changing from one day to the next. I wrote about my desert encounters, about my life, about the red men of the mountains, my friends, the young girl, the sunsets...but little on religion. Religion just didn't hold my interest any longer.

I bid farewell to my protectors and continued my journey!

When I got back to civilization, I sauntered up and down the streets in a warm, light rain that made the sidewalks shine. In and out of bars, cafes, and old apartment buildings, I searched for something that no longer existed for me.

I saw Rudy in his 1940s or 1950s paneled van running every red light, going wherever he would go at one o'clock in the morning; Penny in her broken-down car displaying a sign that read "California or Bust;" and Bob asleep in a barber's chair while a homeless man cut his hair. And I continued picking flowers on the side of the highway like a fool.

What I felt or cared about was only in my dreams now. I no longer yearned for companionship or idle conversations. I felt most times that I was floating on a cloud, slowly moving across the universe.

This place was not for me, so I packed my belongings and headed for the Chiricahua Mountains to find my Apache relatives whom I had not seen in over a hundred years.

I slept in cold desert nights and walked in hotter-than-hell days. I spliced open barrel cacti for water and devoured prickly pear for dessert. It took me a month and a day to walk across the desert floor to the mountain, but I was too late. With their wickiups destroyed, the still smoldering fires ushered the men, women, and children away, without choice, to live on reservations in faraway Oklahoma and New Mexico. The scars of the abused lasting forever.

The fearless warriors with high cheek bones, red skin—the protectors of family and mountains—were now sad, brown-eyed shadows of what they had once been; mere creatures tied with rope, walking alongside the wagons that carried women and children. How they must have cried and agonized over leaving their homes in the beautiful mountains…forever!

How many made it and survived the arduous trip? How many died of starvation? Some survived only to be sustained by the scraps of food their captures tossed at them like animals, and still, others died of diseases they had never known before. How many more died of broken hearts; too numerous to count while their silence screamed sorrow.

My passion for life is gone. My ambition to be a great writer is fading with each passing day, and now is only a figment of my imagination. The love I had for others has vanished like a leaf floating down the river. Because of my very hatred for injustice, I feel more and more discouraged, prompting even a hatred toward myself.

I suppose it doesn't matter. I must continue my sojourn. But rather than walk, I have decided to jump a train and head west. I have never seen the great Pacific Ocean. They tell me the sun sets in the ocean. Maybe I will find for that which my soul is thirsty. Perhaps it is love or friendship; or maybe a good bottle of wine… something…anything. I'm not picky.

In the past three years, I have seen the gods sitting on mountaintops, walking in the desert. On more than one occasion, we talked about the meaning of life. Their faithfulness, kindness, and view of humanity was just too difficult for me to comprehend because I see myself as a sinner looking for deliverance.

Nonetheless, I came to the realization that I was looking for salvation through others instead of looking in the depth of my tattered soul, which had been ravished by heartache. I also found that I have little or no concern for my physical body but have fallen in love with my mystical soul.

But more importantly, I found that I just couldn't compete with the gods because they were not of this world…and I was!

The Red Dress

The Red Dress

I was standing in the living room of my apartment, gazing out of the window onto the dimly-lit streets, people watching, as I tend to do on some evenings, when a yellow taxi #3069 navigated slowly through the narrow cobblestone streets and stopped in front of the brownstone where I live. A thin young woman with stringy brown hair, and perhaps in her late twenties, got out slowly.

She made her way out of the cab, lugging her purse and a large box. The driver of the taxi also got out and started unloading various size boxes from the backseat and the trunk of the cab and commenced to stack each on the sidewalk. I presumed that the young woman had leased the apartment above mine. I exhaled a sigh of relief knowing that it wouldn't be some heavy-footed man.

She wore denim jeans, sneakers, and a loose-fitting white top, and her body seemed to have a perplexing look of emptiness and void of energy. One at a time, she started to lug boxes up the ten steps to the main door and then to the elevator that took her to the fourth floor. It appeared that one box became more cumbersome than the next.

I opened my window and shouted down to her, asking if I could be of service. But there was no response or acknowledgment of my request to assist, so I closed the window, pulled the drapes, and then went back to reading.

Later that evening, before my lights went off, I could hear her pacing the floor. From time to time, I could listen to a soft cry that carried throughout the darkness, akin to silky music from a lonely heart.

The following morning, we rode the elevator together, and she wore a casual green dress, black pumps, and her hair in a bun, a flawless transformation from the previous day. However she never looked up or greeted anyone, spending her time staring at the tiled floor as though counting each square. She was silent and gloomy.

Every day was the same as the last. Then one morning, I managed to say hello, but she never looked at me or returned my greeting, but I saw a faint smile, and I noticed that her eyes were puffy, reddish in color, and were occupied with hurt.

Later that evening before my light went out, I heard her pacing the floor, again with the soft uncontrollable cry. How can she carry so much unhappiness in her heart? Foreboding distress that I was sure prevented her from sleeping placidly. The thought of such sorrow made me feel morose, and I found it hard to sleep.

I was into my studies of Chinese philosophy when I came across a quote that I found apropos, "Tea is a beverage which not only quenches thirst but also dissipates sorrow." So the following morning, with a tremble in my voice, I invited her for tea and biscuits, and she said nothing, that was until we were outdoors. She turned in my direction and in a soft voice accepted my invitation.

"What time would you like for me to come?" she asked.

"How about seven?" I answered.

"That's fine. Oh, by the way, what's your apartment number?"

"It's three ten."

"See you then."

That evening, after work, I rushed to the teashop around the corner from the brownstone and bought Harney & Son Chinese Silver Needle tea and Lotus Biscuits.

As I walked up to the steps to my flat, I could see the lights shining brightly from her apartment, and I became weak-kneed. My body was swarming with excitement, and the anticipation was causing my heart to skip several beats.

I entered my apartment and busily commenced preparing our teatime, and with a burst of vigor, I began to tidy my unpretentious apartment. I was hopeful that she would overlook my lack of everyday cleanliness.

Seven minutes after seven, and I was beginning to think that she would not come and I sat dejected, solemn, wondering if I was too insistent or that perhaps I was not attractive enough or that she felt sorry for me and accepted my invitation out of pity. These were the unanswerable questions that filtered through my paranoid mind.

Nervously, I moved to the window and examined the tree-lined streets in the hope that she might knock at any second. Nothing! I sat at the dining table, poured a cup of tea, took a morsel from the arrangement on the plate, and I ate. The enjoyment was gone, and my sorrow deep, I decided to go to bed and stare at the ceiling.

Late into the night, I was awakened by her, pacing back and forth. I listened to the whimpering that was now part of her nightly ritual. I sat upright in bed, sad yet angry that she made no effort to come by or at the very least slip a note of apology under my door. I slowly fell back incensed and attempted to sleep.

The following morning, we met as usual on the elevator, and nothing was said between us. Annoyed, I stood a further distance from her, and my anger grew with every breath, yet I kept my feeling hidden inside my wounded body. The elevator door opened, and she moved closer to me and touched my arm.

"I'm sorry, may I come by tonight."

"Of course," I said.

"How about seven?"

"Sounds good. See you then."

With a few simple words, my soul was cleansed of all my evil and malicious thoughts. I was overjoyed once again.

That evening, I prepared everything exactly like the previous night, and I sat and waited. At precisely seven o'clock, there was a knock at my door, and I practically sprinted, quieting myself before I opened the door.

My composure in tack, I opened the door, and there she was, wearing a red dress, and her piercing green eyes slicing through my soul. She was more stunning than I could have imagined. Her smile no longer showed the sorrowful hurt she exhibited this past month. I felt relaxed, yet tense that perhaps she might jump up, thinking this whole thing was a mistake and then scurry upstairs to continue her crying.

My nerves were out of control. I asked her to sit on my unsoiled yet frayed sofa. I walked to the kitchen, picked up the tray of tea and biscuit, and then placed the platter on a petite table that rested in front of the sofa. I positioned myself next to her, but I could feel the anxious dampness building on my forehead. I poured the tea and handed her a cup.

This was an uncomfortable circumstance that appeared to last without end. I wondered if perchance I had made a mistake by inviting her to my apartment, but slowly with each word, her shyness began to evaporate, and I became more comfortable myself.

Sit closer to me and tell me about your happiest time, tell me about your family, and tell me the kind of music you like, and tell me what you love to read. Tell me, while I pour you another cup of tea.

She answered everything I asked and more, even about the sadness of leaving her husband who was involved with another woman. Then with a mixture of anger and joyful eyes, she said, "I'm not this flimsy body, you see." I smiled with an apologetic face for having asked so many questions.

We continued talking, and I felt a closeness that I was sure was one-sided, but I couldn't contain myself. Was I so lonely that I could feel this emotional tie with someone who lived in the same brownstone, who I saw on the elevator each morning and by chance a few times in the evening, and who was now sharing tea and biscuits with me? Could this be a fixation that I felt without endorsement? It was late, and she decided to go home.

Later that evening, before my lights went off, I could hear her pacing the floor, and I could still hear the ever-present soft cry. But now I began to pace the floor. My body was full of angst and desolation and knowing in my love-torn body that there was nothing I could do for the girl who wore the red dress.

No contact for a week, and I began to wonder if I had transgressed the boundaries and made a fool of myself. It was about this time that I received a call informing me that my grandmother died. So with trepidation, I packed my suitcase and headed upstate for heavens know how long, but mostly the wickedness in my head worried that I might never see her again.

Upon my return, I noticed the vacancy sign was posted. I jumped out of the cab, and rather than wait for the elevator, I ran upstairs to the fourth floor, and I began pounding on her door. After a few minutes, I realized that indeed she was gone. Dejected, I walked down the flight of stairs to my apartment and noticed an envelope partially under my door.

I unlocked the door then promptly opened the envelope. The message directly read, "I'm sorry, I've gone back to my husband." Disheartened, I sat on the sofa, and I cried like a baby. How sorrowful were her words that could cause me such misery, my heart dismayed beyond mending? The essence of me disappearing with a few simple words, and I felt ashamed that I was thinking only of myself, not realizing that perhaps she was happy once again.

For the next few months, I took my friend's advice and began to socialize more. For the first time in what seemed like ages, I felt a sense of relief, a sense of rejuvenation.

I decided to meet my friends at a neighborhood pub that was in walking distance from the brownstone. There was a chill in the air, so I hunched my back and hurriedly walked into the warmth of the pub. I sat at the bar, ordered a glass of wine, and waited.

With all the commotion and revelry, I failed to feel someone tapping me on the shoulder, thinking that perhaps the pub was so busy that the patrons were merely brushing up against me. That was until I felt a jolt, and I quickly turned.

There before me was the woman who wore the red dress. She asked if we could find a booth. I agreed. So there we were, sitting on opposite sides, and I felt unsettled and apprehensive until she said, "Tell me about your happiest time, tell me about your family, and tell me the kind of music you like, and tell me what you love to read.

At that exact second, if only she knew how much I missed her, but I was too ashamed to express my true feelings. I was still feeling insecure that once again she would disappear, and I would be left alone, alone to stare at four walls that were void of pictures and that perhaps in need of a new coat of paint. But in a manner unsuitable to me, I managed to keep up drivel conversation although internally I was dying to express much more.

I felt more relaxed when my friends finally made their appearance. I became stress-free but guarded, playing with my glass of wine and withdrawing from the conversation, while she, with her expressive eyes, became the hit of the party, which gave me time to crawl into myself. Late into the evening, we said our goodbyes, and I thanked her for stopping by. She held my hand and asked if she could spend the night.

I was embarrassed to say yes because my apartment was what it was when I was alone, shambolic. I capitulated to her beauty and my carnal desire. That evening we were two souls intertwined as one with me feeling an intimacy that I never wanted to end yet to petrified to let go. I couldn't ponder that she might be hurt since my selfish soul knew that I couldn't live without her. And that was the first of many nights when I continued to wonder if by chance I had made a mistake or that she would suddenly leave me. As hard as I tried, I could escape the numbness that would or could eventually destroy our relationship. I reposed in bed, looking intently at the ceiling.

Time passed from winter to spring, and she was now living with me, and I felt a great joy each day as I made my way up the steps to the cobblestone apartment. The thought of seeing her exhilarated me by the sense of being. There was a joist sensation of being able to touch her daily, and my fears of being alone disappeared with each second. Finally, I was able to express myself to her without stuttering or forcing words that now came as natural as breathing.

We strolled through the park, hand-in-hand, and I noticed with an undeniable level of jealousy my protectiveness reawakened by men and women who positioned their eyes on her and murmur degrees of envy. While she, with alabaster skin and piercing green eyes that melted my heart so many months ago, expressing nothing but kindness, and me spiteful with anguish because they knew nothing about her, and I wished that I could be more outgoing if only for an hour a day. Yet I was feeling confident that she was with me and I was with her.

During the day, I spent teaching philosophy to students who were not only squandering their parents' money but also wasting my time by not having a desire to understand the teaching of Lao-Tzu, Machiavelli, Nietzsche, or Descartes. They were simple-minded students whose foremost aspirations were to pass with the slightest amount of effort as possible. This, of course, shouldn't be my disquiet as long as the recompense continues to pay my bills and makes it affordable to me with a good bottle of wine.

Tonight, dissimilar to other nights, we shall go to the coffee shop that provided more than coffee and delivered relaxing jazz, music quiet enough to hold a conversation without screaming at the top of our lungs. Although there were times when I merely gazed at how unbelievable lovely she was even without makeup. She seemed distracted, and I wonder if she might be sick, but upon my inquiry, she just gave me a smile without speaking a word.

The next day, as I entered our Brownstone apartment, there sitting on my sofa was her ex-husband, a poseur who I have met once before. I can feel the blood rush to my head, feeling a tearing sensation, yet I acknowledged him with a pretense of acceptance but pondering what this parasite was doing in my home. And she didn't try to kiss me as she regularly did. This time she was only showing a smile without affection. I sat in my apartment like a total stranger, wondering if I should leave the room or throw him out as the two chatted about this and that, like old friends or current lovers, and me with my elbows on my knees being totally ignored. Finally, turning to me and asking how I have been, then in a split-second excusing himself, and I saw the two profiles approach each other as he gave her a kiss on the cheek then exited our apartment.

The usually calm me, smiling bitterly, no longer seeking to understand, I explode with rarely seen anger. She went into hiding in our bedroom, calling me unreasonable and saying that she was allowed her own friends, which further caused a rage, but I quickly calmed myself before there were penetrating words that can never be taken back and that will survive in the depth of each person forever. I moved around the room like a cat stalking a mouse. Eventually, I gave up the hope that she will explain the situation, such as it was.

I slept on the sofa, and before the lights went off, I can listen to her, pacing the floor, weeping, and I wondered if it was for him or me. I want to apologize, but my innerself ignored the warning signs, and I fell asleep, miserable that she was not next to me. My dreams were full of pity, sadness, and guilt. I was tossing and turning, unable to make sense of what just happened and how it happened, and where was I when it started happening. I was dreaming of the worse because that was what I deserve. I fell into a deep sleep of worry.

I woke up only to find her gone, clothes and all. I couldn't fathom that the one-sided argument could lead to her walking out on me and leaving without so much as a note. Perhaps I was better off not knowing or better off not reading the discourse that I was sure had been developing in her body and soul, chastising me for not being a better provider, paramour, or companion. All I was sure were correct assessments of what I was, yet I sat in this sorrowful apartment lonely and ill-equipped for the torment that I will have to undergo the balance of the day or lengthier. My back ached from my restless slumber on the uncomfortable sofa that should have been replaced years ago.

I dressed in crumpled clothes with no purpose other than to go teach boorish students who I loathe more today than I have the afore-mentioned months. I was receiving blank stares from empty eyes pretending to listen, pretending to learn, and pretending to stay awake. Perhaps she left because I no longer appreciated my skills as a teacher and that my desire to teach has disappeared, like her. The hours until I made my way home seemed to drag on, just like my early years when I couldn't contain my excitement for the arrival of Santa Clause.

I walked up the stairs of the brownstone and noticed that my apartment was uncharacteristically black and joyless, and the brightness was gone. I entered the lifeless apartment, and I felt cold and sweaty. My body was unsteady and terrified that the reality I wished not to experience again was putting an end to the bliss that I thought would last forever. All I could do was brew a cup of tea, sit unresponsively, and listen to the sound of my own weeping.

For two weeks, I slinked by her job with expectations that I might catch a glimpse of her in a disconsolate condition, but to the contrary, she appeared cheerful and filled with joyfulness. I was amble to my sinful apartment benumbed that she has moved on so quickly while I floundered in the sea of self-pity.

I sat in a chair by the grimy kitchen table, trying to compose a letter that will state my regret for having mistrusted her and that perhaps she would reconsider and come back to start a better life.

But in the midst of writing, I found my words insincere and lacking sincerity. I wondered if I truly wanted her back. I walked back-and-forth, trying to be truthful with myself, wondering if I truly loved this woman who I couldn't seem to trust.

I want solitude and time to think of the ramifications of being and living unaccompanied or living with her and the uncertainty that she will once again leave me for the man she truly loved or was infatuated with. Perhaps she didn't know the difference or worse yet that this was what she did because of her own foibles. I reposed in bed, dreading the sleep that will bring dreams of her. I got up and headed to the kitchen instead to finish the letter that never got started.

The following days were misty and dark with the threat of winter creeping through the air and the underbrush and the flora making its last fight to stay in bloom. And the leaves had already fallen, and they gave the trees a scary appearance like tentacles in search of the sun. My apartment's ambiance felt colder than ever before, perhaps it was understood that nothing but suffering, despair, and pessimism subsist in every crevice of this once warm apartment.

I haven't seen her in almost a year, yet I still, for some bizarre, unexplainable way, nurture our time together. If I allow myself to be truthful, I miss the warmth of her body, the touch of her smooth skin, and the taste of her lips.

From time to time, I will see someone who looked like her. I would gape like a voyeur. My mind would be drawing me back to the times we walked through the park or stopped to enjoy a glass of wine while listening to soft jazz, but mostly I sit, daydreaming of the times when I could hold her without question.

I continued to teach, and my attitude has changed dramatically. I have grown a beard, and my hair was long. I now blended in with the students who have accepted me for being cool. Even the female students found me attractive, and I found myself dating quite a few, although there was no chemistry other than between the sheets. When they find out how shallow I was, I get dumped once again but was now a regular occurrence that I was used to and didn't object to anymore.

I had gotten used to the fact that solitude was now my daily companion and haven't seriously thought about her sometimes. I was satisfied with that observation. I didn't wish her anything (good or bad,) and I progressively saw myself as a good guy who was trying to make his way through life. I also saw my friends occasionally, but I didn't make it a point to hit the nightspots or spend my time holding a glass of wine on a nightly basis, preferring the stillness of the night and sitting by the open window of the apartment, people watching and breathing the sweet fragrances of the streets.

I glanced at the far end of the cobblestone street and noticed the silhouette of a woman, leaning beside an oak tree. I wondered if she was waiting for her lover. She began to walk across the street in the direction of my cobblestone apartment, and I noticed that she was wearing a red dress. Whatever, the progress I made to cleanse my notions were now gone from my spirit, and I was instantly filled with a sad rejoice. I tried and composed myself to no avail. I was in love once again.

She knocked softly on my door, and although I attempted to be coy, I stumbled over my feet in a mad dash to open the door. I haven't even given thought to what I will say. I was a twelve-year-old, trying to dance for the first time.

I opened the door and instantly noticed her sad green eyes. She wore no makeup, yet she was beautiful beyond description. My hands were moist. I nervously put them in my pock.

"Please come in," I said.

Without a word, she walked in and moved directly to the window. She turned and said, "I want to come back."

I stand perplexed. My thoughts were leaping in confusion, and my mind incensed by her audacity. My anger wanted to throw her out once and for all, but I succumbed to the weakness that she knew existed within me, and I quickly said "yes."

"I will return tomorrow with my belongings. Perhaps we can talk then."

Then without another word, she left, and I stood by the window as she made her way down the steps unto the sidewalk, never turning back. I felt incomplete, void of any emotions, questioning what I had done.

True to her word, she entered my apartment with a suitcase and several odd-shaped boxes. We sat on the new sofa that replaced the haggard one that I used as bed months ago.

Her voice was soft and calm, and she told me of the mistake that was made when she left but said nothing specific. I dared not asked any questions because I knew not what to ask. She never asked for forgivingness or apologized, and in my thoughts, confusion persisted, but I was happy that she was home once again.

I came to realize that I should die on learning the truth, yet realizing that my love for this woman will never end. And I suspected the day will come when she will again look for a better suitor, and I will be devastated yet again when she walked out the door, but knowing that each time she will return, and I will receive her with open arms.

Perhaps I was a fool or insecure that I was not worthy of another, but I knew that my heart felt a sense of liberation when I lied next to her, and I could hear her breathing softly. This was a feeling that she needed me beyond other men who possibly don't understand her as I do. Who better to care for her than I? And with all her soul, she knew that no one will ever love her as much as I did.

She will disappear from time to time, but the intermezzo will allow her to reflex that her life was with me if only for a short time.

I will get up tomorrow, put on casual clothing, and she a white dress, and we will leave the apartment and go for a stroll through the park. We will have lunch under the cottonwood trees that overlooked the lake. We will watch the white swans make their way from end to the other and unhappy men, rowing canoes while their wife or girlfriends read books or dangle their hands in the water and not once a word between them.

And me, I intended on brushing her silky-smooth brown hair and tell how much I love her while she recited love poems by Neruda. She was aloof with a compassionate but emotionless heart that didn't expose her detached feelings. Even so, I knew she will take care of me, and I will live with more happiness and more gayety than ever before.

Still, I kept her red dress and suitcase in the closet and closed the door. We were in this together for as long as it last because I couldn't seem to find the brighter side of darkness.

The Clock

The Clock

The overnight, featherlike rain made the morning cooler, a welcome reprieve from yesterday's exhausting heat that wilted most of the flowers in the park. Yet, I was confident that the blades of grass still held a remnant of moisture that would inevitably bleed deep into the soil. It was a cry from the floras for that last remaining drink.

I placed myself under the tree, on wet grass, and reflected on my life's journeys that lay deeply in the past. I still had tender memories of spending rainy days, holding your soft hands and talking about the future. Our shoes were soggy from running through puddles, laughing hysterically at everything and nothing. We were filled with joy at being us.

The magnanimous me; with features of the Plains Indians but more resembling my earliest relatives who killed God. Tall, slender, wavy black hair, green eyes, and a smile not seen often; lest I care about you.

And she, rambunctious, fragile with come-hither bedroom eyes. With a sprinkle of joy when she talked about the world with awe and anticipation, she recollected the days from her youth and a displeasure of her parent's breakup but happy nonetheless. The poems she read to me from her tattered book about love and compassion caused me to reflect on my self-image.

I missed those times. How many calendars ago? Just how many sad, if not dreadful days, wondering if someone else held her hand now and talked about the future. And why did it happen, when everything was totally unnecessary, except for the other woman?

I glanced at your picture daily, the one of you wearing the blue swimsuit and the silly smile, while you dried your wet hair. Your image unmoving, resting frameless near the clock, which counted the days and nights without a single word of reassurance. The clock just ticked the time away.

I made my way through the restlessness of each day, dreaming, craving just one more word. I tiptoed for the forgiveness that I was sure would never come, unless the time on my clock cleared a path.

I saw our old friend yesterday. He wore a leather jacket and Levi's jeans, still fitting his skinny frame. His shoulder-length hair hadn't been washed in several days. I was sure. He asked about you and me with no answer except to say that there wasn't enough room for two in my dirty, under-furnished apartment.

I quickly dismissed any more conversation about you and focused on him and his whereabouts during the time that we were together. However, my mind couldn't stay clear of you.

We stood and talked near the huge clock, positioned on a pole near the entrance to a smoke-filled bar. It was a place where I dared not enter, lest I start to drown my sorrows again, like many days passed, the clock ticking noisier than other days, we said our good-byes.

I walked from one side of street to the other and bumped into people I didn't know. I wondered how I got to this place, without knowing just one person, that I could share my life with or impart stories, too. I thought about my friend, who I would probably never see again, and contemplated the times the three of us would go out for a good time.

It was raining. Opaque raindrops bounced from one person to the other, like playing a game of tag, a joke between the droplets. And the clock struck its hourly cry, while the dark cloud cast its heavy cloak on each step I took.

My heart thumped faster and faster, my mind visualized tonight, and the anguish I would encounter once again, while I lay on the couch gawking at the ceiling. The total darkness was in my mind, with incomprehensible thoughts of days so long ago.

I yanked up my shirt collar close to my ears, and I bent forward a bit with my head down as I walked with trepidation. All the while, I was looking intently at the cracks in the sidewalk. My hands were in my pant pockets as I amble to my solitary life.

I managed to fight my way to the rear of the coffee shop, the one where everyone congregated to buy nothing. I sat at an undersized table in the crook of the store, waiting for the rain to lessen. In my confusion, I bought nothing.

Talking without listening, everyone smelled of wet dogs. A young coquette, with painted lips, stringy damp hair and steady dripping tears, forced a smile my way. Apprehensive, I turned and look intently at the rain and thought about you. The coquette, surprised at my action, frowned then blushed.

The clock struck a muted whimper, calling an end to another day, once filled with high expectations. That now floated on the spine of fallen leaves drifting down the river, suggesting and rejecting my attempt to do better yet convinced that my only salvation was to hide.

The clock implied time passing quickly over my body but slowly in my mind. I wonder if I could afford to lose more time, regardless of how annoying I am to myself.

At once, I understand the meaning of this strange visage that are made up of shamelessness and innocence, of beauty once youthful now faded by the clock.

Listen Deeply

Listen Deeply

Eleanor listens closely as her family recounts stories of her childhood. She begins to suspect these are made-up stories to pacify her or perhaps to keep her from learning the truth.

It's never made much difference to her, but lately, she is beginning to wonder why the color of her skin, eyes, and hair are much different than her brothers and sisters. How can this be? she thinks to herself.

Eleanor is also beginning to question why she has more chores than her brothers and sisters. She keeps everything to herself and does what she is told.

Every day is the same for her. Get up, make her bed, wash herself, make breakfast, and get ready for school. The fact that she has to get up earlier than the others and start the breakfast of *chorizo con huevos* is trying at times. Not because it's difficult to prepare but because she has five brothers and four sisters that she cooks for and that is tiresome. Plus, the fact that she isn't getting enough sleep.

In truth, her homework is half-complete once again and that is a problem in itself. How is she going to explain to the teacher (who already thinks she is lazy) that she has all these chores to do before school? Her teacher probably has heard stories like this before. Why should she believe her?

Eleanor prepares herself for more punishment. She would rather the teacher give her a spanking than be kept after school.

Getting home late and missing her chores is a call for more punishment. Either way, today is not going to be a good day, but lately, she hasn't seen many good days. She wishes her dad would come home soon.

When she gets home, she immediately takes off her school clothes and hangs them up. She can't afford more wrinkles or get them dirtier because these are the same clothes she has to wear all week—that is, unless one of her sisters lets her borrow one of theirs, which is highly unlikely.

She has just enough time to read a few pages from her favorite book—the one she has read over and over again and keeps hidden under her pillow. She reads fast, because soon Eleanor will have to help in the kitchen.

After serving everyone their dinner, it is finally her turn to sit and relax. She knows that she is on-call. When one of her brothers or sisters asks for seconds, it's her job to serve them more. She eats standing up. This is a habit she will take to adulthood.

Friday night! Eleanor goes to bed tired but happy because her father is coming home tomorrow. She is excited and can't sleep.

The anticipation is too much. She says a few prayers, hoping that this might help her sleep. They do. She sleeps peacefully but is up before the sun rises.

Eleanor puts on her tattered and stained play clothes and darts out of the house. She is not afraid of getting in trouble for not doing her chores, because she knows that her father will protect her from her mother and anyone else. No one hurts her when her father is home.

Eleanor runs up the steep mountain trails with all her might, and she finds a spot where there is a perfect view of the valley. Off in the distance, she can see a man walking on a worn-out trail, with knapsack over his shoulder. He wears a straw hat and a red bandana around his neck. She knows instinctively that it is her father. Don Refugio was a miner in his native Mexico. Since coming to the United States, he prospected gold to make living for his family. He spends many days away from home in the rugged mountain for the gold nuggets that he keeps in a coffee can. Although close to all his children, Eleanor is his favorite.

She races down the mountain almost falling but regains her balance and continues running at full speed to meet him. He is all smiles as she jumps into his arms. "How was your trip?" she asks in a grown-up manner.

"*Estuvo bien,*" he says. "*Y tu Como estas mi chica?*"

"I missed you so much," she answers.

She holds his rugged, strong hands tightly and they make their way home. It is a ritual they will continue for many years.

When at home, Don Refugio spends his time tending to the garden and feeding the chickens. In the evenings, he sits on the porch, rolls a cigarette, and whittles dolls for the girls and carves toy guns for the boys.

After many years in the mines and panning for gold, Don Refugio develops arthritis in his hands and back. This illness will make him bedridden for the remainder of his years. Eleanor's brothers are older now and have jobs to help, as do her older sisters.

At fourteen, Eleanor still does much of the housework and continues to cook all the meals for the family. She is in charge of making *tortillas y frijoles*. Her schooling is getting much harder, but for unknown reasons, her teachers is more understanding of her situation.

School has ended and Eleanor is sent to live with relatives in Golden Gate, "*Un barrio en Phoenix.*" Her tio y tia will pick her up and take her to Phoenix, where she will work in the cotton fields.

On Saturday, the day before her fourteenth birthday, her tio y tia arrive. Sadly, no one mentions her birthday. Only her father wishes her a happy birthday. He gives her a Saint Christopher necklace to wear.

Eleanor finishes packing her clothes in a flour sack and places it in the back of the beat-up blue truck, where she will ride. It will take four hours before they reach their destination. Eleanor puts on the hat her dad gave her and sits clutching her flour sack. She is not concerned that her family doesn't pay attention to her. For Eleanor, this will be a vacation.

Eleanor arrives at her Tio's and Tia's house. They take her to the back of the house where they have a rollaway bed in a closet-sized room. Eleanor has nowhere to put her clothes so she leaves them in the flour sack. The room has a musty smell. The bed has a sheet that used to be white and a tattered blanket that looks more like a well-worn *serape*.

The next morning, Eleanor is awakened by a loud command from her *tío*. "Eleanor, get up it's time to go to work." She gets up, washes, puts on her work clothes, and heads for the kitchen to eat breakfast of *tacos de huevos*.

After breakfast, Eleanor and her cousins Lucy and Joe start their walk to the cotton fields. The fields are a mile from Golden Gate. They arrive at the starting point where all the workers are given instructions for the day. Each is issued a six-foot burlap sack for the cotton they will pick. Eleanor, Lucy, and Joe take their sacks to the fields where they will begin the grueling, backbreaking work.

Eleanor is placed with the more experienced workers. Los hombres will show her how to pick the cotton. Eleanor is excited. She watches and does what the others do. On hands and knees, dragging her sack, she begins pulling cotton bolls. It doesn't take long for her back to become sore and her fingers and hands blistered and hurting, but she moves on. At the end of the day, she makes $0.75. It is the most money she has ever had.

After work, instead of going back to the house in Golden Gate, Eleanor, Lucy, and Joe make their way to a tiny woodshed. It holds six cots placed on dirt floors and a small wood-burning stove. This is where they will make their home for the next three months.

Late in the evening, they sit around the fire, cooking *una olla de frijoles, y Chile rojo y tortillas*. Eleanor listens to more stories of her family. She learns of aunts, uncles, and cousins she never knew existed. Her oldest cousin Lupe, whom she doesn't like, seems to know everything about the family. She recounts stories of the old days and how family members moved from one place to another in search of work.

Lupe talks about the relatives who died along the way and the ones who survived. She tells yarns about *los pueblos* where they lived, *la comida* they ate, *los bailes y los guapos jóvenes*. Each place is more exciting than the next. All these stories are interesting but unsettling. Why hasn't anyone told her about aunts, uncles, even cousins she has never met? Are they ashamed of these family members? Eleanor thinks.

After dinner, she walks to the canal that flows a quarter mile from camp and draws water to wash the tin plates and forks they were all issued on their first day. She mustn't lose any or they will have to pay the owner.

When everything is done, she crawls in her cot. In some crazy and strange way, she is happy. She counts her money over and over, and finally puts it in a tin can. She hides it in her flour sack. It is summer, but the nights are cold; she wraps the blanket around her and falls asleep.

The next morning comes early. Eleanor sits up and finds that her entire body is sore and achy. Her hands are blistered and finger-nails chipped. The mosquitos have also invaded her body. Bites are everywhere. Nonetheless, it's time to get dressed and go back to the fields. She grabs a couple of *tortillas con mantequilla*, drapes the six-foot-long bag over her shoulders, and walks to the field.

Day in and day out, the same routine. Some days, the owner provides warm water to drink, and other times waits until lunch time, which is usually fifteen minutes long. With the hundreddegree-plus days, Eleanor finds herself weak from not drinking enough water. She never complains.

Payday is usually Saturday afternoon. That means that Sunday, the men will make a trip to one of the *barrio* stores and buy beer, sodas, and meat that will be cooked for everyone in camp. There is a cost. Eleanor chips in twenty-five cents, a third of her daily pay.

The most confusing thing about this whole summer is that everyone in the camp uses the same outhouse, and each person is allowed but one shower per week. On Sundays, everyone gets up early and lines up to take their shower.

Eleanor enjoys Sunday afternoons. Each and every one in camp is having a good time. The men sit and smoke cigarettes, drink *cerveza*, and play their guitars, while the woman prepare *Baracoa con Chile Verde, frijoles, y tortillas*. Sunday afternoon and evenings are the same. From time to time, the men and some woman have too much to drink, and fights and arguments occur. Nothing serious, just petty disagreements about who lives in the best part of the city. Eleanor sits quietly as declarations are made implied about who lives in the best barrio, is it Golden Gate, *Las Milpas, El Campito,* or *La Sonority?* It doesn't bother her because these locations are as foreign to her as Mexico or Canada. But she does like to hear about other places.

Just before the end of the summer, the nightly after-dinner talks are getting more meaningful. The details of family members are now the focal point. Taking center stage are the gossip of family drunks, thieves, and of the children born out of wedlock. Eleanor listens deeply and begins to realize Lupe is getting to the point she wanted to make from the beginning of these chats, like a puzzle that you should have figured out by now. Still confused, Eleanor is not certain what they are getting to.

Finally, without concern of any one's feelings, Lupe, the main storyteller, blares out, "Why do you think you look like you do?"

Bewildered, Eleanor looks around as though the remarks are directed at someone else. Lupe points her finger directly at Eleanor and says, "You! Yes, you!" Eleanor sits there in shock. The heat from the fire seems hotter, almost burning her skin.

"What are you talking about?" asked Eleanor.

"Haven't you ever wondered why you have lighter skin than your brothers and sisters? Why you have blue eyes and red hair? Don't you know that your real father was an Irishman who sold pots and pans door to door? *Eres estúpida,*" says the jealous Lupe.

Everyone begins to laugh. Eleanor is stunned and runs to the shack, throws herself on the cot, and begins to cry profusely. Her head is spinning. She feels betrayed by everyone, especially her mother.

Her last day in the fields, Eleanor can't feel the pain in her back or hands. Her mind is somewhere else. Clouded with everything she has learned, she can't muster a smile, even when receiving her final pay.

They tell Eleanor that she is a good worker and hope that she will return the next summer, but Eleanor doesn't bother to answer. What started as a good experience has suddenly turned into the most dreadful incident of her life. *How could they do this to me?* It is her last thought as they leave the camp.

Eleanor, Joe, and Lucy walk back to Golden Gate, and no one said a word, especially the loudmouthed Lupe who has joined them, although not welcomed.

Even back at her tio and tia's house, Eleanor is treated differently from the first day she arrived. She retreats to her little room and begins to pack. She lies in bed refusing to eat and waits for morning to come.

There is no one to greet her when she gets home. It doesn't matter because the only person she cares about is lying in bed sick. She drops her flour sack and runs to his bedroom. She gets down on her knees and, with tears in her eyes, gives him a big hug. "Look, Papa, I made twenty-five dollars!" He beams with joy. However, he can see the cuts on her hands and arms, and it makes him incredibly sad. "*Me hija*, that is money you earned. Save it, you will need money to buy school clothes."

Many years later, after having her own family, Eleanor still thinks about her dad and misses for him deeply. She thinks how hard he tried to protect her from that thing she would learn one day. She also has come to understand that he knew from the beginning that she was not of his blood, but, in his eyes, she was his, more than the others.

One day, I asked my mother about her childhood. With a gleam in her eyes, she told me of all the wonderful things she did and learned from my grandfather. What a magnificent and caring man he was. But she never mentioned my grandmother.

Just One More Time

Just One More Time

I continued walking with a limp after jumping from the railroad trestle and twisting my ankle on the solid floor below. If I hadn't leaped, perhaps I would still be high-stepping with a smoother gait and with more spirit instead of this sluggish ambulatory staggering.

As far as my eyes could see, nothing appeared to be moving in the immensity of the wilderness. Yet I knew that life subsisted even under the red rocks that covered much of the desert floor, along with the pitiful half-eaten wildflowers protruding beneath the stones. Nonetheless, I continued my slow walk and followed the setting sun while the glaring rays penetrated my swollen eyes.

Just yesterday, my life was perfect, except that I didn't have a job, or a place to live, or a family, and certainly no money. So why did I have a perfect life? Because I wasn't dead! Although from time to time that was exactly how I felt, dead!

On this arduous journey, all I did was think. I thought about the most ridiculous situations that made no sense even to myself, the thinker. Like realizing that most of my friends attended schools elsewhere, who cares? From time to time, mainly during the cold nights, while sitting on the hard ground, I stared at the twinkling stars and deliberated the good times. But without haste, I disregarded the walk down memory lane when my stomach began to growl with a vengeance. And rather than feeling sorry for my predicament, I rolled over and fell asleep.

Considering everything that happened to me, I felt fortunate in many ways. Yet I wonder about what could have been, especially when it came to me, nursing the bottle that changed my attitude about survival and the pursuit of happiness. Could my life be better without me?

The heat in this uncompassionate place has brought on a flashback about her. That perhaps she wasn't picture-perfect, but I whispered that she was to the point of going out of my way to be altruistic. I was to be as genteel as I could be, never mind her wicked, self-centered ways, and that she cared about someone else while being with me. I cursed the ground that she walked on, but I found myself coming back for more or less of whatever she dished out. But slowly, my withered mind began to face the inevitable that perhaps I was just lonely.

I continued my unobtrusive walk with the sun beating down on my balding head and buckets of sweat pouring down my already blistered face. I tenderly wiped away the wetness from my eyes and saw an unidentified grayish wall.

There was a wall that ran for miles in either direction. I meandered toward the obstruction and immediately stopped when I see hundreds of men, woman, boys, girls, and even babies, forcing their way over the perilous wall. They have their tattered knapsacks, hanging from their shoulders, garbed in unfashionable clothes, and wearing shoes that don't fit, all the while yelling and screaming, pushing and shoving with tears in their eyes, not from sadness, but the tear gas being hurled at them by men in green uniforms. It was repulsive chaos.

I turned and ran in the opposite direction, afraid of the mob or police, whichever group reached me first. I disappeared behind a Saguaro cactus. However, my lungs were filled with tear gas and desert dust, and I couldn't breathe. The lack of oxygen caused me to faint, and I fell to the desert floor, hitting my head on the red rocks with such force it split my head open, blood gushing unendingly in every direction.

I woke up in a car, rocketing a hundreds miles over the speed limit with my unwashed hair, flying uncontrollably in every direction. The driver was a young and alluring splendor with red hair and deep blue eyes and wearing a light blue dress that exposed the suntan on her shoulders who was seemly unfazed by her surroundings, including me. All the time, the driver was holding a cigarette in one hand, and cell phone in the other, leaving the car to drive itself.

She stopped at a diner in the middle of nowhere. The restaurant was surrounded by cacti and two gas pumps, showing the price of gas at twenty-five cents a gallon, an unreadable sign having fallen to the ground, partially covered with sand, spider webs, and gossip of something better inside.

We entered the rundown diner and sat in a booth with torn leather seats. There was an uninviting table covered with crumbs and the sight of the occasional brown roaches, scurrying from the kitchen to the main floor in pursuit of a gooey dessert.

She ordered the house special for the two of us without ever looking at my eyes or my withered body. The waitress, wearing a pink dress and matching apron and hair stacked a foot above her head, brought us two secondhand cheese sandwiches and a three-day-old coffee. It was the best meal I never had. We ate in silence. My perfect-bodied driver paid with a handful of pennies and left a single dollar bill on the table that I took and put in my pocket when her back was turned to me.

We got in the car, and she accelerated with such force that her wig sailed into the sunset, which caused me to laugh, although she didn't blink an eye or seemed to care. She turned her head slightly in my direction and asked if I remembered her, and of course, I lied and said yes.

"Do you remember the first time we kissed?"

"I feel miserable and wished I did but don't," I answered.

"It was under the cottonwood tree," she said.

I turned and took an in-depth look at her, and I began to weep with sadness, but moreover, I felt elated like confetti on New Year's Eve. My body felt lighter than a cloud. I asked her to pull over. She stopped the car in a cloud of dust. I leaned over and kissed her hard, and she died.

I left something cooking on the stove. The aroma was drifting from one room to the next, and then I realized I didn't have a house. The suspicious me also discerned that my shadows were huddled in the corner, conspiring their escape. I angrily gestured for them to leave my eyesight. Who desired ingrates like them anyway? They're followers who were continually initiating difficulties for me when all

I wanted was peace and quiet. Fuming, they left through the back door of the house that didn't exist.

At last, summer was coming, and I, for one, will be thrilled to shed the five layers of clothes and lie on the red rocks on this unforgiving desert. Perchance the sun will paint my albino skin. I might even rid myself of my graying beard, although I was beginning to enjoy how I looked. It gave me a distinction among the desert vermin.

There was a possibility that when I get back to the city, I will call my nurse friend, and we can go dancing. She, all of five-foot-ten, with short blond hair and blue eyes and killer curvature, and "man" she can dance and drink, not necessarily in that order. I knew she will be eager to see me, and I was sure she would want to pay for everything, including my new attire.

She took me to Mel's, an overpriced men's clothing store. Mel was a short man with a round face and squinting eyes. Not a nice person. He handed me a cup of tea with his fat-dimpled hand and pretended to like me, but I knew otherwise. It didn't matter.

I bought a black tuxedo and white shoes, and my nurse friend paid. We went dancing from the dark night until daybreak. Exhausted, we departed to her apartment. She vanished into the bathroom to make herself more presentable, and I crept out the window.

Nothing ever appeared as it seemed. Some days, I lived in the desert, while other times, I stayed in the desert; but mainly I didn't live anywhere.

I've learned a hard lesson in my life that it was never about leaving there, but it was all about being here. And so I continued to trek throughout, doing without, just one more time.

A Strangers Request

A Stranger's Request

This is an incredible story to write or even tell anyone. But someone out there has to understand that things like this happen. It doesn't make me a nut as most people already believe.

It was May of 1972, and I drove from New Mexico to Monterey, California. The weather was perfect as I made my way on Interstate 10. Not a cloud in the sky and traffic, except for the occasional semitruck, was almost nonexistent. I decided to roll down the window and let the cool air hit my face. It also kept me from falling asleep. I turned up the radio and began to sing in my best Frank Sinatra voice to "Summer Winds."

My first stop was Blythe, California, where I filled up with gas. My hope was to make Los Angeles by dark. After a fifteenhour drive, I pulled into a Holiday Inn in Hacienda Heights. I spent the night and got a good night's rest. Tomorrow, I would be headed north on Highway 1 to Monterey.

The following morning, still tired from a restless sleep, I was anxious to get started. I checked out of the hotel and headed to the nearest restaurant for breakfast. The next stop was Phillips 66 to fill up one more time and was off. What I forgot to tell you is that as I crossed the desert, I noticed a man, hard to tell how old, walking on the side of the road. He wore a gray wool coat with patches on the elbows, black pants, and black fedora. His backpack hung over one shoulder, and he carried a walking stick. What I found odd was that he was walked in the desert with no inclination of wanting a ride. He just walked with stooped shoulders. He looked directly at the ground as though looking for something.

I bring this up because as I was getting gas, I saw the same man walking on the sidewalk across from the station. At first, I couldn't believe my eyes. Surely, it couldn't be the same man.

But there he was walking, looking down at the sidewalk, still looking for whatever he lost.

I was not sure what came over me, but I walked across the street and asked him if he needed a ride.

He looked up me with empty eyes and said, "What makes you think I need a ride?"

"I don't know, I just thought."

He cut me off and asked where I was going.

"I'm headed for Monterey."

"In that case, I will allow you to give me a ride. However, I don't want to talk, and I will not answer your questions."

I agreed but had second thoughts. I think I just felt sorry for the old guy. "Let's go," I said.

I began to drive on Highway 1, anxious to get to Monterey, two hundred miles away. He sat close to the door, as though suspicious of my driving, or worse that he would jump if I said anything that displeased him. I drove for twenty miles in complete silence. No radio on either. I took in the beautiful scenery. Suddenly, he asked me what I did for a living. It came as a complete shock. I couldn't think. You would have thought he wanted me to explain the making of the atomic bomb. All of a sudden, my brain started working again. I said, "I'm in sales." That was it for another twenty miles. Again, out of nowhere, he asked me where I was from. This time, I answered without hesitation, and that was it for another twenty miles. By this time, I was getting really nervous. I was afraid to say anything. My knuckles were white from the grasp I had on the steering wheel. I was uncomfortable from sitting in one position, too scared to move. He turned in my direction and said, "Relax." The weight of the world lifted from my shoulders with that one word.

Big Sur was five miles away, and this would be the last chance to get gas, buy a soft drink, and maybe a few snacks. More importantly, use the facilities. I pulled over and asked if he needed anything. "I would like a Coke. If you don't mind, I'm going to walk for a bit. Do you mind waiting?"

Big Sur is bordered by the Santa Lucia Mountains on the right and the Pacific Ocean on the left. He chose to walk toward the Pacific Ocean. There were trails all over, but I wondered if he had been here before or if he was just exploring. I also thought that this was my big chance. If I had any sense, I should run into the store, or buy my goodies, run back to the car, and/or drive off as fast as I could. But I said, "Sure, take your time." Was I nuts? This guy could be a sicko criminal, and here I was being this nice guy. I made the most of my wait. It gave me time to unwind and drink my pop and eat my Twinkies, while he was out doing whatever he was doing.

When we started off again, it was back to the silence. We reached Carmel-by-the-Sea and said, "Hey, I'm ready to get out."

"Is anything wrong? Monterey was still about thirty miles away," I said.

"No, this is far enough."

Then I saw him reach in his coat pocket. I thought this was it, a knife. If it was a knife, he would slide it between my ribs, and I would be finished. Instead, he brought a worn yellow envelope. He looked at it for a second and then gave it to me. He said, "Please don't mail this letter but take it to the person whose name you see on the front. Can I count on you to do this thing?"

"Sure, I will do as you request."

He got out of the car with neither a thank you nor a good-bye. I sat in the car as he walked off. His head down, staring at the sidewalk. I took a look at the name on the envelope and the address. I had to deliver this envelope to the other side of the country.

It would take me two years before I could deliver the letter. Every time I got close to the name written on the envelope, it seemed that she had moved. Once, I was one month short of finding her. Toward the end, all I had was her description. I was told that she had remarried so the name on the envelope was no good to me.

I kept searching. One day, I was stopped for running a red light. While the officer processed my driver's license, I asked the officer,

"Do you know the person whose name appeared on the envelope? Maybe she lives in the vicinity?" I asked.

He took a long look at the letter. He asked, "Where did you get this letter?"

I told him about the man and the ride I had given him, the whole story. He stared at me for the longest time and finally said, "That's my mother." In a stern voice, he asked, "How did you get that letter?"

I said, "Believe me, Officer, the story I told you is the truth. I have been looking for her the past two years."

"I can have the letter," he said.

"I'm sorry, but I have to personally deliver it. That was part of the agreement."

He did not give me a ticket, for which I was extremely grateful but insisted that I follow him.

I followed the officer to the outskirts of town, down a one-lane country road, with cornfields on the right and row houses built after the Second World War on the left. Some of the houses were well taken care of, while others had seen better days. We passed an abandoned schoolhouse, with an abandoned play yard now covered with weeds as tall as a car. Her house was situated on the corner two blocks from the old school. It was well maintained, with white picket fence and garden with every conceivable variety of roses, something Rockwell would have painted.

The officer led me to the front door where his mother waited for me. Apparently, he had called her from his police car and briefed her on who I was.

She opened the door and, in a gracious manner, extended her hand and introduced herself. Her hands felt rough, probably from gardening. But she had the most amazing smile—a smile that made me feel at home, an unpretentious smile, a smile that most people wished they had. "Please sit," she said. "Would you like something to drink? I just made some iced tea."

"That sounds terrific," I said.

She looked at her son and said, "Why don't you go back to work? I'll be all right."

"Are you sure? I can stay if you like." He gave his mother a kiss and said, "I will call you later." On his way out, he stopped next to me and gave me a look that said, *If you hurt my mother, I will break every bone in your body and then throw you in jail.*

I understood the look.

"Always concerned, aren't they?" she said.

We sat in silence for a while. I couldn't take my eyes off her. Her hair was a silvery white, with eyes the color of the sky, no makeup on the alabaster skin, and that smile. "I understand you have something for me?" she asked.

"Oh! Yes!" I took out the wrinkled envelope from my pocket and handed it to her. Her hands quivered. She stared at the envelope for a minute or so. She seemed almost afraid to open it. "Perhaps I should be going," I said.

She looked at me and said, "No, please stay." She opened the envelope. The letter was but a single page. She read and reread the letter. Then she closed her eyes. When she opened them, I could see the tears. She read the single-page letter again. The tears started to roll down her cheeks. I felt terrible. I didn't know what to do or say. So, I just sat.

Whatever she felt. I didn't understand. Whatever she thought, I had no comprehension. My life was simple and I was void of emotion, but this was getting to me. Deep down inside, I didn't care for other people's feelings, but I found myself vulnerable to the tears on this total stranger's cheeks. As one who is always prepared, I didn't even have a handkerchief to offer.

She looked up at me and said, "He was a good man. He was thoughtful. He had lots of energy and was the life of the party. That's how we met. I was with my girlfriends at a Fourth of July party, and he came up and asked me to dance. We danced all night. It was wonderful. He was an excellent dancer. In fact, after we got married, he made it a point to take me dancing every weekend. He called me his 'Ginger Rogers.' She tried hard to hold back the tears, but it wasn't working. She told me about her husband. Everything she said was good, almost like nothing bad had ever happened in their lives.

But why would he be somewhere else? I thought.

It was about this time that the conversation finally hit a wall. She told me, "My husband had his own business. It was a gasoline station and tire repair shop that went under. He lost everything, including their home. He just wasn't the same. He went from job to job and from one rental property to the next. That she took two jobs and tried to help but he became resentful. He told me, 'That no wife of mine has to work.' But things went from bad to worse. Now I knew why I couldn't find her.

"Finally, after two years of misery. He told me, 'I have to go west. I hear they are hiring at the shipyards in Los Angeles.' So he packed his bag, and I took him to the bus station. He told her, 'I would send for her and the boy once he got settled in.' Tell me about him. How did he look? Did he seem happy?"

What's to say? I thought. *That he looked like a bum? That he wasn't a good man?* "Well! We didn't spend much time together, but he seemed in high spirits," I said. "He was heading to San Francisco to work for the railroad. I don't know what he looked like before, but he was on the thin side, nicely dressed, and had a good wit. He did mention a 'Ginger Rogers,' but I just thought he had seen one of her movies lately."

A lie with every breath. I don't know if she knew I was lying or that she just felt better because of my lies. Would you rather I told her the truth? Why should I be the guy, a total stranger, destroying the vision she had in her mind. So, I continued my lying.

We talked for a couple of hours. It may have been longer. She got up and fixed me a chicken salad sandwich and poured more of the delicious iced tea. We talked about this and that, and I came to find out how strong a woman she was and the hard work it took her to get to this place. I felt good that I had come to know her.

When it was time to go, I said, "Would you mind if I kept in touch?"

"I would like that very much," she said. Instead of shaking my hand, she gave me a hug and said, "A good liar you're not but a good man you are."

Crazy story! I told you it would be. So, was it true? Did I keep in touch? More importantly, how could I turn down "a stranger's request."

Hey Joe

Hey, Joe

An Epic Tale

Joe sat brooding on a threadbare couch after having been recently discharged from the US Army. He was disenchanted by the repugnance of war and attempting to piece his life back together while staring at the flames dancing in the fireplace. The physical aches of the shrapnel embedded in his back were made worse by the chilling winds blowing downward from the Swiss Alps. Nothing, however, could liken the pain to that of his first and only love, Mary Katherine.

From his cabin window, Joe saw his new home of Murren, Switzerland, a community of eight hundred people, the majority of which were farmers. He observed the cows and goats roaming and grazing freely on the mountainsides. Pine trees dotted the village, and clouds hovered over the little community like a coverlet.

The evening lights glowed from every house throughout the valley as families gathered for their meals. Joe, meanwhile, stood in the kitchen; Joe, slicing pieces of bread and cheese and placing it on a wood table, positioned to the right of the roaring fire. He sat down to eat and read, only to find himself distracted by the ever-present visions of Mary Katherine and his mother. Dealing with a bottomless sadness he had never experienced before, even while fighting in the trenches, Joe tried to clear his worried mind. He descended in to a deep sleep.

Joe was born in Cleveland, Ohio, on October 23, 1897, to a rich industrial tycoon, Big Joe and his wife, Mildred. Joe was born a preemie whose chances of survival appeared slim. Without sleep and with constant prayers, Mildred cared for him night and day, until little Joe's health improves without complications.

The spindly but precocious Joe, by age three and to everyone's surprise, could count to one hundred and recite the entire alphabet. He was already making great progress in reading at this tender age. Joe's life would evolve with one accomplishment after another.

Big Joe, beaming with pride, often took his son to perform in front of his pals or whoever else might frequent in the neighborhood bar. "Hey, Joe! Show all these fine people that you can count to one hundred and that you know your letters," bellows a boastful Big Joe.

Joe, unaware that his dad has made side bets with the nonbelievers, stood up on a wooden crate and began to count to one hundred before proceeding to recite the entire alphabet. When finished, the spectators cheered at the small child's endeavors…despite their losses. Big Joe passed his top hat around to collect the money owed him. Joe's reward was twenty-five cents and a pat on the head.

As time passed, Joe's skills in the classroom became legendary. Joe was the brightest and most liked student in school. If it had not been for his mother's insistence that Joe live a normal childhood, Joe would have jumped one grade and possibly two.

In quieter moments, he roamed the woods behind his parents' mansion. Although Joe thought of his home as just a big house with an even bigger backyard, he enjoyed the solitude of the outdoors. He walked in a meaningful way through trails he carved out by trampling the green grass. Most times, he ended up tracing the stream that snaked its way across the massive backyard. Joe sat on the bank of the stream, staring with single-mindedness at the water, clear eyes following the leaves that float by, wondering where they came from. Hour upon hour, Joe earmarked his time in this fashion.

Meanwhile, Big Joe made it a point to invite prominent dinner guests. They were people of power and great reputation.

Sometimes, the mayor, city councilmen, senators, congressmen, and, on special occasions, even the governor would attend Big Joe's soirees. Joe positioned himself at the far end of the huge table, picking at his food, listening to the big people talk, and understanding every word of their conversations. If the discussions centered on politics, Joe had an opinion. If they talked about finances, Joe understood even though he never said a word. Joe was only ten years old.

By the time Joe is ready to graduate high school, he had grown tall with the body of an Adonis. Joe graduated at the top of his class. Big Joe assumed his son would attend Yale and seek a law degree before entering a career in politics. Joe, on the other hand, had different ideas and enrolled at Ohio University to study Greek Philosophy. A disheartened Big Joe, worried that his son was wasting his talented mind, exclaimed to his wife. "How in the world he is going to make a living?"

"He will be fine," answers Mildred.

Nevertheless, that was what Joe wanted and so, four years later, he graduated with distinction in Greek Philosophy.

War had been raging in Europe since 1914, and Joe contemplated his future. On the sixth day of April 1917, the United States entered World War I, eventually known as the War to End All Wars. Unsure of what to do, Joe did as he had done so many times over the years: He walked in the woods behind his home. Ambling in solitude without direction, seeking an answer, Joe pondered whether or not to enlist. What made matters so difficult and confusing was that Joe now had a girlfriend, Mary Katherine, whom he did not want to leave.

Their whirlwind romance caught everyone off guard. The tall debutante with blond hair and bedroom eyes had men clamoring for her attention. It was the mild-mannered Joe who got her affections. However, from the beginning, the spoiled Mary Katherine made demands. But in the end, after much thought and despite his sorrow, Joe opted to enlist. Mary Katherine expressed her anger but supported his decision with a stipulation that they marry as soon as he returned from the war.

He enlisted in the Army and, because of his outstanding aptitude scores, was sent to Officer's Candidate School. After six months at OCS, Joe was commissioned as a second lieutenant and assigned oversees duty.

The night before Joe left, Big Joe and Mildred hosted a going-away fete. Everyone of any prestige was invited. Joe was unaccustomed to all the attention, preferring to spend time with Mary Katherine in the rose garden. He tried to make Mary Katherine understand his role in the war, but she was aloof and emotionless, choosing instead to go indoors. Joe felt an uneasy pain in the pit of his stomach. The next day, Big Joe, Mildred, Mary Katherine, countless supporters and the town band gathered at the train station as Joe boarded the New York Central. Joe, uttered good-bye to Big Joe, hugged his teary-eyed mother, Mildred, and tenderly planted a kiss on the cheek of his tearless and still angry Mary Katherine. He boarded the train, waved a final goodbye, and made his way to the main cabin to find his seat.

It occurred to Joe for the first time, as the train rolled of the station, that he might never return. His mind began to fill with uncertainty. Joe looked out of the window as the train made its way along Lake Shore, passing Lake Erie, and tried to take in as much of the scenery as his mind could capture. The train continued south to Williamsport, Pennsylvania, for a thirtyminute stop to pick up passengers. He got out to stretch his legs and inhale much needed fresh air, then back on the train, as it chugged eastward past Newark, New Jersey, to its final stop in Brooklyn, New York.

Joe would deploy from Fort Hamilton on the first day of June 1918. He and the other soldiers would board the "Leviathan," formerly the German passenger liner *Vaterlund*, whose destination was France. Fourteen days on the open seas with moments of heaving every meal overboard, Joe was anxious to feel terra firma.

As the Leviathan gets closer to France, all troops were told to stay quiet and put out cigarettes and lights. The disembarking point was Saint Nazaire, France. The landing had been kept a secret because of German U-10 submarines and German Curtiss Model AB-2 dive bombers that traverse the area, like scavengers looking for their next meal.

Joe reported to headquarter command center. "I understand this is your first assignment?"

"Yes, sir," he answered.

"Well, it, won't be easy, son. So, take the bull by the horns," said the commanding officer.

Joe saluted the commanding officer and stepped outside to meet his new infantry regiment, who themselves were no more than several weeks out of boot camp.

They stood at attention as Joe hollered out, "We are headed to the front without delay. Let's get rolling!"

On a hot and humid day, while his countrymen celebrated the Fourth of July, Joe and his regiment see combat for the first time at the Battle of Hamel. Fighting from trenches in the open fields of Le Hamel, a quaint town in norther France, the battle lasted but ninety-three minutes. Yet, twenty-six of his troops were killed. Joe sat in the mud-filled trench with several bodies positioned next to him. Joe lit his first cigarette ever. He inhaled, almost choked. He began to assemble dog tags and began to write letters to the mothers and wives of those who had died that day, not two days after arriving in France. Joe did not know how to explain or explain these wrenching events.

His first taste of war and death made the mild-mannered Joe calloused. Once, while he walked sluggish in the dead of night to the end of the trench, Joe stumbled over something. He struck a match to look down. It was a headless body. Frightened beyond description, Joe lost control and began to laugh with tears streaming down his cheeks.

After the Battle of Hamel, he and his troops headed for the Argonne Forest where the loss of soldiers had been heavy for the US and French troops. He marched side by side with his infantry on the well-worn muddy roads. The ruins of farm houses, uprooted trees, trucks, and jeeps burned along with the carcasses of mules and horses littered the countryside. A disgusting odor drifts through the air of the once pristine countryside. American and French soldiers who had fought in the Argonne Forest sat on the sides of the road with dead eyes. Joe and his troops marched by feeling depressed and anxious.

As they approached the Argonne Forest, the noticeable shell-pocked earth gave way to the forest, with trees of all shapes and sizes. Ravines, hills, meandering springs, thick underbrush, and dense ground fog allowed visibility of only twenty feet.

Ahead were German trenches paved with barbed wire and supported with machine guns' nests, poised to shower rounds at anything that moved or made a noise. Joe gave orders to his lead sergeants to ready the troops. "Advance at thirteen hundred hours!" he commanded. His troops huddled around a cluster of pine trees and began to get their rifles in shipshape condition by cleaning, reloading with full magazines, and attaching bayonets. They waited. Some of the men commenced praying. Others lit cigarettes, and some adjusted their boots. Nervous tension exists among all, but no one talked.

At precisely thirteen hundred hours, Joe gave the order to attack. In swift uniformity, the troops struck. Their orders—to wipe out the machine guns' nests. The simultaneous blast of a thousand guns were ear-piercing. The troops were surrounded by the thick darkness of smoke, floods of flames, and brightness from mortar shells. Countless men fell, never to get up again.

The sounds of screaming and wailing pierced the air as the streams ran red. Joe's regiment suffering many hardships, including the loss of numerous lives. Twice, Joe was blown off his feet by the violent jarring of bursting shells.

Thirty days of nonstop fighting led to a shortage of food and water. Torrential weather forced Joe's troops to seek shelter in hurriedly made trenches. His troops huddled shoulder to shoulder and covered themselves with rain-soaked woolen overcoats. The lack of sleep became a torment. Men slept standing up, like horses. A silent cough existed. The infantrymen were dying of hunger and thirst. Joe and one of his sergeants began to crawl under enemy fire to a nearby stream where they filled their canteens. On the way back, the sergeant is hit in the leg by machine gun fire. Joe proceeded to drag him and canteens to safety. To make matters worse, his troops were now running low on ammunition, and the communications with his superiors seemed nonexistent.

A continuous barrage of artillery fire showered down and turned the night to red. Shells came close, their shrieks raised to an unbearable pitch before they burst. Joe and his troops hugged the sides of the trench for protection as bits of steel hummed over their heads, and dirt seemed to fall in buckets.

Somehow, after months of fighting, Joe and most of his battle-worn troops had survived. Nonetheless, war left Joe with many distorted views and questions. Was war necessary? What about the senseless killing? Is war for politicians? The war plagued Joe. He would never be the same person after the Argonne Forest.

Joe's personal agony was translated in the letters he wrote to his mother and father. Mildred cried herself to sleep every night. Meanwhile, Big Joe found solace in his fifth martini of the evening. Neither consoled the other.

But Joe's letters to Mary Katherine seldom mentioned the horrors of war. His letters were buoyant with an expression of love in each word. He talked about their wedding plans when he returned home. He wrote about the house they would live in and the many children they would have. He managed to overlooked his surrounding when he wrote to Mary Katherine.

After six months of constant battle, a shell-shocked Joe and his infantry troops were given a much-needed R&R. They anxiously headed to Spain, where mail would be waiting. "Hey, Joe! You've got a letter," called out the clerk. After he retrieved the letter, Joe, nervous with excitement and just able to cross the threshold of a local bistro, tore open the letter from Mary Katherine. "Dear Joe... this is the most difficult letter I will ever send you, but my love for you demands only honesty..." He didn't know if he could sustain the courage to continue, and so he looked up into the sky as a frantic means to summon strength. Mary Katherine would marry another. A million tiny pieces of rose-colored stationary littered the entrance to the bistro as Joe, shocked and confused, stepped a slow walk to headquarters.

On a cold bitter day on the eleventh day of November 1918, the war came to an end. Joe, still saddened over Mary Katherine's pronouncement, decided not to return to the United States but instead began a search for a home somewhere in Europe. After much deliberation, he elected to make Murren, Switzerland, his new residence. Back home, Big Joe expressed his anger while Mildred's tear-streaked face could not hide her broken heart.

There are two routes when entering Murren. Joe could go by either the narrow-gauge railway or walk on a restricted dirt road that clung to the mountainside. He chose to walk. The marks embedded in his mind make him timid to the people who encircled his daily life. He walked with caution, careful not to trip on a rock that would send him off the mountain. With a future filled with ambiguity, Joe pressed forward.

Joe entered the small town and observed English soldiers at the Hotel Alpenruhe as they prepared to board the train. He later learned that English prisoners of war were directed from Germany to Murren. The English prisoners would then be repatriated back to England.

Joe strolled into the post office, entered, and was greeted by Hans Bruner, the postal clerk. "Schoen tag," says Hans.

"Do you speak English?" asks Joe.

"Ja," replied Hans.

A sigh of relief flowed over Joe's face.

Joe then began to spell out all his needs as he paced back and forth. He needed for a postal box, a nice cabin, clothes, and food. On and on he went without catching his breath. Hans listened with patience, then told Joe to sit and have a cup of tea. "We will talk more when you relax," said Hans.

Joe was relieved after his talk with Hans and walked to the Hotel Alpenruhe, where he spent the night. That evening, Joe was full of excitement. He went to bed and for the first time in what seemed a lifetime, he slept in peace. The next day, he rose early to settle all his business. By midafternoon, Joe was now the proud owner of a cabin in the Alps and the newest resident of Murren, Switzerland.

Joe rambled to his cabin nestled in the footsteps of the Swiss Alps, with supplies in hand. He hoped to lead a simple life of reading, hiking in the mountains, and writing to his mother, but never a mention of Mary Katherine.

Two times a day, Joe strolled unassuming to town for his breakfast and dinner, walking over pastel carpet of gold clover, bellflowers, milk kraut, and daisies. Joe was always polite but never engaged in conversation. The people in town knew that Joe was an American war hero, but no one ever asked him for the time of day, let alone invite him to social gatherings or inquired details of any personal nature. He was somewhat of a mystery, spawned by rumors spread by the townspeople. On occasion, the village people stopped by the restaurant to glimpse him eating his breakfast or dinner. To the small village of Murren, Joe remained an enigma, and he seemed to prefer it that way.

Each morning, Joe followed the same routine. He would pack his book of poems by Gertrude Stein, Joyce Kilmer, Amos Wilder, and Alan Seeger in his military-issued backpack and headed for town. He would walk on the paths and narrow lanes, with head down, seldom looking up. He would enter the restaurant where the waitress, accustomed to his hermitlike behavior, seemed on impulse to know the routine. Joe's meals were always the same.

They consisted of a pot of hot tea and honey, bread, butter, and marmalade. Breakfast was presented in silence while Joe read from his books. Joe never looked up. Joe paid when finished, then walked home. He seldom ate all the bread, preferring to save a slice or two in his backpack for the menagerie of creatures who waited uncomplaining at the cabin their daily snack. Suffice to say, Joe's comfort resided not in the conversation of the Murren community but in the solitude of his own existence and the company of his animal friends.

By late afternoon and before sunset, Joe packed his book of poems in his backpack and headed to town for his dinner; his routine remaining unchanged. Dinner consisted of a pot of hot tea with honey, roasted chicken, potatoes, carrots, a plate of cheese, and one cookie. Yet again, Joe paid, and saunter home without speaking to anyone.

One day, while walking home, Joe noticed the bakery open longer than usual. He crossed the cobblestone road and stood peering in the window. Behind the counter was a beautiful woman with blue eyes and blonde hair. She turned and gave Joe a smile only beautiful woman can give; it was enticing.

The smile sent Joe back to the day he met Mary Katherine. The overwhelming, intoxicating, wicked flirtations, visage of an angel. He stood with his foolish thoughts—thoughts of youth. He gazed back at the woman in the bakery and without acknowledgment, he puts his head down ashamed at what he was thinking and walked slower than was his standard, pondering about the woman in the bakery.

Once a week, Joe found himself walking by the bakery. He never entered, just looked at the beautiful woman from afar. She turned and gave him a sweet smile with her eyes, and he felt guilty for no reason. He did not respond but instead wandered down the cobblestone street to question why his courage had disappeared, all the time wondering what Mary Katherine has been doing these past eleven years.

On Tuesday, the twenty-fourth day of October 1929, the world plunged in the Great Depression. Millions lost their entire savings. For the rich, it meant losing their fortunes, and Big Joe was one of them people. Unable to cope, Big Joe took his own life and left his wife Mildred with their home and jewelry. Nothing else.

Joe received a letter from his mother that explained the entire situation. Joe was morose and decided to visit his mother. However, before he had time to arrange to go home, he received a letter from the family attorney to inform him that his mother has expired from a heart attack. Joe felt angry and guilt-ridden. "How selfish my life has been," lamented Joe.

Fifty years have passed and Joe, now in his seventies, had long white hair and a beard to match. His life was now on slow motion; everything took longer. He still packed the tattered, worn book of poetry in his thousand-times re-stitched military backpack. He headed for town. It had not altered much, except many of the stores and the restaurant owners had died, and the beautiful woman in the bakery had since married and moved to another town.

The curiosity of Joe's youth had long faded. He was now just an old man walking, stoop-shouldered, with cane in hand, to go to a restaurant twice daily to eat. Even the new and young waitresses at the restaurant didn't know who this strange fellow was and why he never talked to anyone. They wondered why he always ordered the same food. Why wasn't he married or have children? What did he do in the cabin by himself? Gossip, gossip, and more gossip, carried from one young person to the next.

During winter, Joe looked out of his cabin and still marveled at the pine tree branches heavy with snow and the stunning white blanket that covered the village. He looked at the Alps with reverence. The Alp peaks were crowned in brilliant snow and the cliffs changing hue every hour. Years of living a hermit's life, Joe feeling vindicated and the happiness from his youth finally brought a smile to his face. He no longer reflected on Mary Katherine. However, rumors of an impending storm threatened Joe's quiet existence. He rushed to town, nearly falling on the snowpack path. He entered the restaurant that sat nearly empty and waited for his dinner. Joe ate in haste and scurried to his cabin just in time to hear the growl in the Alps. It became darker than normal, and the rumbling moved closer to his cabin. Joe sat untroubled in his sofa in front of the fireplace and anticipated the storm to pass like it had so many times over the years. Louder and louder, it roared like a freight train out of control, getting closer and closer. The storm-caused avalanche expanded, picked up steam, and covered everything in its path with snow and debris, including Joe and his cabin in the Alps.

Two days after the disastrous storm, the people of Murren were still excavating the cabins on the mountainside. Men looking through the ruins for survivors or bodies, while Hans, the postal clerk and the only friend Joe had made, began to rummage through the bags of mail, trying to salvage as many of the soaked letters as possible.

There was commotion outside. One of the village men ran in the postal office and yelled, "They found the American's cabin!" Hans jumped from his seat, grabbed his wool coat, and wobbled to the site where the villagers were digging. Hans waited as they cleared the snow and hacked down the door with shovels. He and a few of the older men entered the distressed cabin. They noticed stacks of books that covered the cabin floor. They discovered Joe sitting on the well-worn sofa in front of the smoke-filled fireplace. They called out his name but no answer. The men walked with caution to where Joe sat. They glanced down and there was Joe with *Tender Buttons* on his lap, frozen in time. The men walked out cabin, soundlessly crying.

Back at the post office, Han's eyes were drawn to a pink envelope with extraordinary penmanship. Hans picked up the letter. It was addressed to Joe. With copious grief, Hans placed the letter in Joe's mailbox. The letter was from Mary Katherine.

Mexico

Mexico

It's the first day of January 1965, at approximately two in the morning. The biting wintry weather has dipped below freezing. I'm nineteen years old and running through a city in a country I know nothing about, running for my life. I'm crisscrossing streets and into alleyways that are mostly dark at this time of the morning. Sprinting on primarily unpaved roads in a city, I can't even pronounce. I don't know north from south or east from the west, but more importantly, I don't have an inkling how to pinpoint the American border crossing.

I'm darting up and down dimly lit pothole-ridden streets, in and out of filthy alleys, ducking in store doorways, hiding, and afraid of every passing car. I'm sucking in the icy cold air that has started burning my lungs. Each step worse than the last, once even finding a patch of ice that sends me tumbling to the ground. My face meeting the frozen ground with such force, that I stagger to my feet dazed. My growing fear is that I won't make the border before I'm caught. I put my hands on my knees to catch my breath, and I notice a hole in the knee of my pants, and my hands are muddy and bleeding. I can't worry about my appearance, I have to continue running.

Of all the things that could happen in my life. Running through the streets of Agua Prieta, Mexico, on the coldest day of the new year, trying to save myself is not what I expected. I accepted an invitation to spend the holidays with my girlfriend's family. My inexperience telling me it would be fun.

But with all the complexity, I began to think that perhaps I made the biggest mistake of my young life. The night's freezing air is causing my eyes to water, or perhaps they are tears.

To better help you understand my unfortunate circumstance, I have to take you back seven years to where it started.

I was twelve years old. My cousin is having her thirteenth birthday party, and my friend Bobby and I were invited. It was a typical party with music and dancing. Still, it also had a Mexican tradition that I knew nothing about...but I was about to find out!

A beautiful girl with eyes the color of the sky and red hair walked up to me and cracked a confetti-filled egg on my head. Of course, I was taken back, but I understood later that breaking a 'cascarone' on someone's head was a sign of good fortune, as well as a sign of affection, or mild flirtation. It was no big deal at the time. Still, it would be the beginning of many Mexican traditions and customs that I would come to discern over the years, and that eventually be my downfall.

When the party ended, we made plans to meet at the movies the following Saturday. I was looking forward to seeing her again and spent the week daydreaming in each class. It seemed that Saturday would never come. Finally, we met as planned, and we sat close to the screen. With a bit of encouragement from my bud's, who were there for verification, I proceeded to make my move. I put my arm around her shoulder, leaned in, and kissed her. She jumped out of her seat and ran out of the movie theater. It would be seven years before I saw her again.

After graduating from high school, I decided to attend a college but opted out after my first year to enroll in a barber school in Tucson.

I moved in with Rod and Dwight, buds from my hometown. Sometime in September, I was introduced to Bob, who graduated from Salpointe High School in Tucson. One weekend, Bob took us to a school dance at his alma mater. The gym was packed. I stood towards the back of the gym and did some people watching while listening to music. I noticed a stunning woman walking in my direction. My first thought was she didn't seem to fit with the other girls, she was way to elegant for this group. The way she dressed and walked, gave her a sophisticated appearance. She also resembled some I knew but couldn't my finger from where or when. Finally, I came to me, she was the one I met at my cousins' party, some years back. By the time I realized who she was, she disappeared into the crowd.

The following day, I was talking with one of my buds in school who lived in Tucson. I asked him if perchance he knew my old friend. I gave him a full description, and without missing a beat, told me that they graduated from the same high school and even told me where she lived. Excited, I started combing through the phone book, and I found her family's telephone number, and later that evening, I called.

That was the beginning. She met me at school, and we talked briefly. The next time I called, she invited me to meet her parents. Her parents were born in Mexico and, in many ways, continued to practice many of their old customs. Which I knew nothing about. Her father was your typical "macho" dad and seemed to rule the household with an iron fist. Her mother, on the other hand was more genteel, an attractive woman, and was an incredibly gracious person. I liked her mother a lot.

From the outset, her father didn't like me, mainly because I didn't speak Spanish, or perhaps that I wasn't good enough for his daughter. Or both! Her mother, on the other hand, thought that I was relatively good-looking, with green eyes and all, and seemed more accepting of my shortfalls.

I never officially got permission from her father to date his daughter, but we saw each other anyway. What did I know? I do believe that her mother was okay with our relationship. Or, perhaps I was wrong on this matter as well.

Anyway, her parents were going to spend the Christmas holidays in Mexico, and I was invited. Why I was asked and why I accepted is still unclear in my mind. I suppose I just wanted to spend time with her.

The family in Mexico seemed to be close-knit. Most lived relatively close to one another, and they appeared to people of means. Her uncle's house, where we were to stay, was well maintained and nicely furnished. To be quite honest, I'm sure what I was expecting or what they expected of me.

I was introduced to all the family members. The men eyed me with apprehension. The women, well, again, what did I know? In those days, I thought everyone liked me.

After the introductions, to my best recollection, I was led to a room with ceiling fans. I remember sitting on a wood chair, facing some women who would be my inquisitors. They, of course, were polite, but I didn't understand two words that were spoken to me. I felt droplets of sweat hit my trousers. I tried to answer, but I went brain dead. It was at this time that I began to question why I made the trip. My comfort level disappearing by the minute. I just didn't know how to act.

I don't remember talking Spanish to my parents as a youngster. It was something they did with each other. Although, I suppose my siblings and I learned through listening. Still, our conversational Spanish was non-existence. But here I was, a million miles from home, in a place I didn't belong. I just stared at everyone, trying to smile, then I began to realize that perhaps my buddies were right when they called me "coconut. Brown on the outside, white on the inside." It became apparent that I didn't fit, and that didn't make me feel good. I felt dumb.

Enter the men who didn't care if I was handsome or not. They just wanted to know if I was a man. So, in front of the women, they ask me to go to the red-light district. I decline. The men were offended in more than one way. First, I have rejected their offer. Secondly, I have refused in front of the women: an absolute no-no! I failed my manhood test.

It was New Year's Eve, and the entire family was getting ready to go to her uncle's night club. We went, but soon, she and I found the party rather dull, or perhaps it was just me. My preference was to be with people of our own age. So, I called my friend Oscar who lived in Bisbee, USA. Oscar invited us to his party. The first mistake, we borrowed her dad's car without permission. We scurried across the border, where we party until after midnight. The second, blunder, was coming up.

When we got back to her uncles' house, we were greeted by the entire family of uncles, aunts, cousins, and of course, her parents. The women grab her by the arm and drag her to another room, and I'm told to sit. One of the uncle's proceeded to give me a piece of his mind, that somehow or another, I fully understood.

I was neither afraid or concerned for my well-fair. My only thought was for her and how she was being treated. But there was nothing I could say or do that would change the situation. I couldn't even apologize. I've screwed up. I'm also thinking about how uncomfortable it's going to be when we head home.

My brain running in all directions. I kept thinking that my unfamiliarity with the customs of this country would cause grief and pain to her family, perhaps even shame. Even the repercussions to her at a later date. My mind spinning out of control. Here I am, in another country, and I'm the ugly American.

I look at each member of the family, and all I can see is hatred. I'm beginning to think that they will be beating me at any moment. I wonder if I should defend myself or just let it happen? But what if, I strike back? Then what? But the most extreme circumstance would happen. I was totally unprepared for what would transpire next.

"You have thirty minutes to get out of this house and to the border. If we catch you before you reach the border, we are going to kill you."

"What about my clothes, I ask?"

"You are leaving with nothing except what you are wearing," they say.

"Can I at least get my coat?" I ask.

"You have thirty minutes," they answer.

I get up and brush past two of the men and out the door. I stop at the curb and look right and left; I opted for the left and take off running. My mind is a complete blank. All I can think about is getting to the border.

I begin running through shadowy roads not knowing north from south or east from west or more, importantly, in what direction the American border gates are located. I'm running up and down the streets, in and out of alleyways, and ducking in doorways every time I hear a car.

Breathing the icy cold air that is beginning to burn my lungs, stepping on a patch of ice that sends me tumbling to the ground. With torn pants and muddy hands, I get up and start running again.

Twice I see her father's red Buick and, in the nick of time, manage to duck in a doorway. Once I even threw myself on the cold frozen ground. I am sweating in freezing weather.

I used to deliver newspapers in my home town. I would get up at four in morning and walk to a gas station to retrieve my papers, then packed them in my bag. I trekked up and down canyon streets, over mountains to the next canyon all without a flashlight. I had to dodge cacti and pray that I wouldn't slip on a boulder and fall. I delivered papers for three-years, and in all that time, I was never afraid. I suppose because sooner or later, I knew that I would get home. But here I was in Mexico, in a city I knew nothing about, running for my life, and I'm nineteen years old. What a bitch!

As I got closer to the border, I had no intention of stopping. The Mexican border guards ordered me to stop.

"Alto, alto, they scream," but I kept running.

They rushed after me, waving their arms, yelling at me to (alto) stop, but I continued, paying them no attention. I ran past the security gate and into the American side. I was met by two American border patrol officers who were driven out of their warm office by all the commotion outside.

I was taken to their workstation. I sat on a steel chair, and they gave me a blanket and coffee. I recounted my story to their doubtful ears. To give more credence to my narrative, I pointed to the red Buick parked at the gate on the Mexican side.

I would spend two weeks with my friend in Bisbee, with no money and wearing the same clothes. No one knew where I was. When I finally got back to Tucson, I learned that my godfather/uncle passed away. It would take some time or me to mend the broken fence, I now had with my dad. It would be years later that he found out why I didn't go to the funeral, that he gave me a wink, assuring we that were okay.

She and I continued seeing each other and eventually got married. If I have one regret is not ever talking to her about the incident. I didn't know what happened to her on that day. I didn't know what kind of punishment she experienced or what else she faced at home, and that bothered me. It troubled me for years. I wish I could have been more forthright, perhaps it would have been good for both of us to talk about that night. Perhaps it would have prevented my resentment.

Ironically, her father and I made peace, but it was many years later. She and I divorced, but when I was in Tucson, I made it a point to stop and visit him. He always had a smile for me and me for him. He always said how thin I was and that I should eat more. I talked to him in my broken Spanish, and he seemed to understand. I was also there on the day he died.

For me, it was an experience I will never forgot. Perhaps in many ways, I came away with a better understanding of the differences between people on that cold and freezing morning, so many years ago.

In my studies of Taoism, I quickly learned that "even in the midst of an extreme situation, the wise are patient. Whether the situation is illness, calamity, or their own anger, they know that healing will follow upheaval."

Taoism has also taught me to understand and appreciate the differences that the world bids. That all opposites are part of the same entity. So, that's how I live, one day at a time.

Farewell

Farewell

After three years of symmetry and two years of unyielding quarreling, the honeymoon is over for Penelope and Steven. The relationship everyone envied has died. Timid Penelope, with her dreams of being in a picture-perfect relationship and being a respected writer, gone. The overbearing, ambitious, and sometimes cruel Steven seems to be the main cause. After five years, the day has finally arrived.

"Farewell" Penelope says as she boards the train. She is carrying only a small leather suitcase in one hand and a white handkerchief in the other hand that she is using to wipe away the tears that are running thick down her cheeks.

"Farewell." Steven waves. *Farewell, wow! That sounds so permanent. I wonder if that's what she meant to say?* Steven thinks to himself.

Penelope walks slowly to her assigned seat, still crying but not once looking back. All she hears is the porter calling, "All on board," as the train pulls away from the station.

On his drive home, Steven begins to reconstruct the constant arguments. He is beginning to feel glum, wondering how he could have dealt with the situation better. "I didn't even kiss her good-bye," he laments.

The long drive home, made even worse by the bumper-to-bumper traffic, is making his feelings turn bitter. Steven begins to blame Penelope more than he does himself and is glad they never married.

"I have a good job," Steven says aloud. "I know it requires travel, perhaps more than I like at times. Nonetheless, it is what I do. It's my job!" Steven continues griping, his voice drowning out the music coming from the radio.

"She ought to be grateful, not having to work. What an ingrate! It would've been nice if she cleaned the apartment now and then.

Or washed the dishes instead of just sitting in front of the typewriter banging on the keys. The next great novel? What a joke! She didn't even cook me a good hot meal," Steven says defiantly!

The more Steven thinks, the madder he becomes. His blood boiling. Farewell! Good riddance is more fitting. Steven is driving heedless, darting through a red light, and narrowly missing a man on a motorcycle.

Penelope sits staring out the window. Her mind lost in confusion and hurt as the train thunders past fields of flourishing green grass, passing the small town with a single streetlight, where she went to school. Penelope knows that her home is not far away. *I wonder what kind of reception I will get from mom and dad?* she ponders. I hope they don't tell me, "We told you so." What will I do now? Penelope falls asleep, waking only when the train roars to a stop.

Penelope's dad greets her at the train station. He gives her a big hug and knows on impulse that she has been crying but says nothing. They get in his old red pickup truck and ride home in silence.

Penelope can see her mother Mildred waiting at the front door. With tears flowing from her eyes, Mildred says, "Oh, my poor baby." She holds her daughter with tender love, like she did so many years ago. "Let's sit in the kitchen, and I will brew you a cup of tea. Dad will put your suitcase in your bedroom."

An uncomfortable situation and silence between the two. "What are your plans?" asks her mother.

"I am not sure," answers Penelope.

"You just take your time, everything will be all right," says her mother. More silence.

After dinner, Penelope sits on the porch swing, staring at the stars, hoping for a miracle to ease her pain. She replays her version of why things went wrong and wonders if she could have been more understanding. What if he calls and wants me back? What shall I do?

The phone rings and Penelope jumps up from the swing with anticipation. Her heart pounding only to find that the call is for her dad. She goes back to the porch swing and rocks back and forth, staring at the million stars in the heavens.

Steven is back at the condo, pacing the floor. Talking to himself, "Should I call or not? If I call and she answers, what do I say? I'm sorry would be a good start. On the other hand, it was not all my fault so she should call me."

Days become weeks, weeks become months, and months become years. Penelope and Steven talk on occasion, only to see how each is doing. Steven promises to visit, but something always comes up at work and he never goes. Penelope is saddened, if only for a second. She then becomes angry, throwing her hair brush, cracking the glass on her vanity. She begins to weep.

Forget and forgive. Penelope and Steven have moved beyond their problems. Now their conversations center on careers (mostly his), the weather, and the people each is dating. Nothing serious for either. There is still something there, but they never discuss their true feelings; it's just known.

Steven talks about his most recent promotion as sales manager and the new places he travels to, once even calling from New York. Penelope is excited for him and is a constant source of encouragement, wishing him well.

On a rainy and gloomy day, Steven realizes that Penelope is the one for him and he calls her. Penelope answers and after a brief exchange, she says, "Steven, I am going to marry a boy from my hometown. His name is Bill and is a school teacher." Penelope doesn't wait for a response from Steven. She says, "Farewell," and hangs up. Heartbroken, Steven goes out and gets drunk!

Days become weeks, weeks become months, and months become years. Penelope never finished the next great novel, but her children more than make up for whatever literary success she dreamed of in her youth.

Steven achieved all the financial success he sought. However, he went through countless of unfulfilled and unsatisfying relationships that left him depressed. Steven now sits in his rocking chair glaring at the stars, feeling sorry for himself and agonizing, wondering how much better his life might have been with Penelope. Disheartened, Steven mutters farewell and jumps off the terrace.

Laugh When You Rather Cry

Laugh When You Rather Cry

The storm passed, leaving the streets of Lisbon slimy and teeming with rubbish. In a nearby bar, which reeks of stale cigarettes, the stocky bartender marches to Pablo de Esquellas's table and says, "Either settle your tab now or get out of my bar."

Pablo, with wavy black hair that hasn't seem a comb in weeks and wearing yesterday's clothes, looks at the bartender with venomous eyes and clearly agitated. He says, "Out of my way, you Neanderthal, you are blocking my view!"

"You're drunk, pay me what you owe me or get out!" bellows the bartender.

Pablo throws a peseta at the bartender. He picks up the coin monetarily satisfied. Pablo continues his painting, but nothing worthwhile is pouring from his brushes.

Demoralized, Pablo begins tearing one page after another from the pad and throws them to the floor. "Why don't you go home and sleep? Perhaps your mind and eyes will work better tomorrow," suggests the bartender.

Pablo reluctantly gets up from his table, staggers, and says, "You are right. I shall go home and sleep." Pablo begins to walk unsteadily on the slippery and uneven cobblestone streets to the winding stairway that leads to his room a short distance away.

It's been three years since the once-promising artist left his beloved Madrid. He left his wealthy family rather than surrender to the Alhambra Decrees that forced Jews to leave Spain or convert to Catholicism. "I'm a Jew, and no one will make me convert," a rebellious Pablo tells his parents. Pablo de Esquellas packs but one bag for clothes and a satchel for his art supplies, begins the arduous five-hundred-kilometer walk to Lisbon where they will accept his kind.

Pablo walks handsomely to Toledo. He walks in a small inn where the locals are eating and drinking. His sits at a corner table but immediately feels apprehension. The barkeep brings him bad wine, foul-tasting water, and day-old chicken, a tolerable meal. That evening, he sleeps in a rather suspicious bed. The only thing for breakfast is chocolate. Before leaving Toledo, Pablo buys supplies of lentils, potatoes, apricots, figs, and bread.

The early morning is misty and dreary. Pablo is greeted by an old man who tells him to be extremely careful on the road. "There are robbers who have no mercy." Pablo thanks the old man and continues to walk cautiously, looking at every unrecognizable moment on a road that appears more like a footpath.

Morning, noon, and night, Pablo walked with anticipation. Rationing his food, sleeping under trees, sometimes in hay lofts... the walk continues. Over rocky surfaces, covered almost entirely with a forest of cork trees and exhibiting in several instances of picturesque views. Through rich and pleasant countryside and finally through pines, shrubs, and sandy soil, he wears out one of his finest leather boots. Pablo finally arrives in Lisbon.

Pablo enters Alfama, the Jewish Quarters, where there are adequate and inexpensive rooms. He reaches the Arco de Rosario with its poorly lit narrow streets, laundry which hangs from windows, and bars where singers perform mournful songs.

Although granted asylum in return for payment, Pablo realizes too late that the Portuguese government has decreed the enslavement of all Jews if they had not yet left the country, unless they must convert to Christianity. Pablo is befuddled and outraged. After months of going underground with other Jews, Pablo succumbs to the decree and he converts.

Nothing in Pablo's life is the same. Depressing nights of drinking ancient muscat wine are now his steady friends, as are the thieves and whores from the slums that are now his home.

Every morning, with a pounding headache from the previous night's carousing that threatens to undue his creative mind, Pablo grabs his satchel, easel, and paper; he strolls to the waterfront to paint the extraordinary imagery of the people and their day-to-day struggle to carve out a suitable livelihood for their families.

With a mangy dog by his side, Pablo begins to paint, experiencing sorrow for the misfortunates like himself who are no longer permitted to exercise their religion. They are not enthusiastically accepted by the faith that they have to adopt. Pablo paints the abstract people, questioning if there might be a better life elsewhere.

That evening, Pablo returns to the bar with the argumentative bartender. He sits and awaits the next confrontation, but instead the bartender tells him of a job. He alerts Pablo that the city of Lisbon is searching for someone to paint a mural in the municipal building on the plaza. Pablo drinks only one *copa de vino* and gives a slice of bread to the filthy dog. He walks home upright without stumbling.

It's Wednesday morning. The air is chilly, and Pablo walks with shabby coat, wrinkled shirt with tie, and tattered pants into the municipal building. After several hours of interrogation from city dignitaries, he walks out beaming. He has been commissioned to paint the mural. The theme is beauty and absolutely nothing political is allowed.

Pablo walks throughout the Jewish Quarter, taking notes and drawing on a pad with pencil. He remembers the days in Madrid and the treatment of Jews. Pablo is ready and eager to begin painting the wall painting.

The defiant Pablo begins to paint the fresco. He uses images of wealthy noblemen and politicians tossing Jews from their homes, imprisoning them, inflicting pain. He depicts slums, anguish, misery, the crucifix, the star of David, the Holy Land, and Portuguese Inquisition as his predominant but perilous theme.

Six months go by and Pablo finally finishes. The big uncovering would happen at noon today with city dignitaries, the wealthy from throughout the countrysides. Anyone of prestige would be present. The mural entitled "*Reír Cuando Lleras*" (Laugh When You Rather Cry) is revealed.

A harsh gasp overcomes the crowd. "Sacrilege, they scream." The mayor orders the sentries to immediately arrest Pablo. The following day, confined Jewish workers carrying cans of black paint cover up the "*Reír Cuando Lleras*," and Pablo is imprisoned. A week later, Pablo de Esquellas is marched to the plaza and hanged in front of the desecrated mural.

The Rainy Day

The Rainy Day

I find a tan Coach purse on the train and like a thief, I examine everything within—a billfold with twenty dollars and loose change, a half-empty pack of cigarettes, and photographs. I wonder which one is you and who are the others. Fire-hot lipstick, the sweet fragrance of perfume, and only a business card showing your name.

I drive the shining slick roads, going to the address on the business card, driving through an older but more affluent part of the city where three-story brown stone homes line both sides of the street. I park on the sidewalk next to the well-lit house. I sit with the sprinkles of rain skipping on my windshield, staring at the silhouette dancing carefree to music I can't hear. My mind races and like a voyeur, I can't keep my eyes off the stunning swaying of the shadow on the wall.

I get out of my car, the rain beating down on my head. I hurried on the cobblestone pathway leading to the front door, with my eyes glued to the window, hoping for a glimpse. She's reading while the raindrops fall ever so tenderly on the tin roof, carrying the sounds of children dancing, frolicking carefree. It suddenly changes as the raindrops become more unmistakable pounding images of a looming storm. The temperament of the day changes from peaceful to guarded, then uneasy seeking healthier shelter, you leaving your book of poems resting next to your half-empty glass of wine.

Waiting for the rainbow to appear, God's assurance that everything will be all right, while you ease your way back to your safe place surrounded by soft downy pillows. Your half-empty glass of wine, back to the poems that make you feel worthy, looking for the certainty that hides in your kindheartedness.

You are awakened by the thought of others who seek what you have, with some jealousy, some with hunger. There is more merriment now and less distress as you go back to search, yet painful, the truth that you struggle, deprived of crying. What have you learned from the teachers who have discovered what the heart wants on this rainy day?

My eyes entirely still, my body petrified, or knock. "This must be your purse?" Sadly, the shadow seems unreal. Captivating beautiful to the touch of babies wanting to be caressed and held tightly, but morose, like the rainy day.

Ever since that night, I sit all day at my desk and know from that lone meeting that my heart lacks joy. I find myself daydreaming, sensing the bouquet of her perfume everywhere, even on my clothes. I wish that I could be the one she dances with and reads to on those rainy days. Once or twice a week, I drive by her house hoping that her husband isn't home.

Thrill

Thrill

Friday morning, another successful week, but he is feeling exhausted. As much as he likes traveling, this week has taken its toll on his mind and body. Of course, it's nothing he cannot overcome. Before he heads to the airport, he makes one final stop at the Park Central Mall, where he will treat himself to a couple of new ties and a pair of Cole Haan loafers. His personal reward for a job well done.

He makes his purchases, then decides to do some window shopping. He still has plenty of time before his flight that leaves at nine. He walks, moving slowly from one window to the next, not really interested in anything in particular, just enjoying the solitude and rethinking the week and how he can improve.

He passes a women dress shop and notices a mannequin dressed in a light blue dress. It catches his attention. He stops and stares at the dress. He doesn't know why. It's just striking and reminds him of someone but doesn't know who. Perhaps it's taking him to another place in time. He stands there for what seems like hours.

Suddenly, out of nowhere, he hears a voice calling his name. He comes out of his self-induced trance, turns around, and there in front of him is a very attractive woman with shoulder-length blonde hair, sky blue eyes, and an alluring smile. "Wow!" she says. "Is that really you?"

He's caught totally off guard and doesn't answer. He just examines her, trying with all his might to recognize who she might be.

In a very awkward moment, he extends his hand and says, "It is really good to see you," still unsure who she might be. All the while, she is going on and on, and he is not hearing anything being said. He is just trying his hardest to recognize her. Suddenly, it occurs to him that they dated many years ago.

Suddenly, he cuts her off and says, "What a thrill it is to see you." He leans over and gives her a big hug. He takes over the conversation.

They stand in front of the women dress shop until he finally asks, "Do you have time for coffee or tea?"

"Yes," she says with great excitement in her voice.

They walk to Le Bistro, a coffee shop not far from where they are standing.

"How long has it been?" he asks.

"Well, I'm not exactly sure, maybe thirty years," she answers.

"So, tell me what have you been doing?"

She starts out by telling him that she was married once to a deadbeat guy. That she has no children. And she is now a professional painter.

"What type of paintings?" he asks curiously.

"Oh, I do landscapes, personal portrait, and on occasions, abstract paintings. I use all mediums—watercolors, oils, and pen," she says.

"What an exciting profession," he says.

She is all smiles but seems rather embarrassed.

They continue their conversation, and he is steadfastly fixed on her every word. His mind beginning to drift back thirty years to the first time they met.

It was at Encanto Park in the spring of 1971. He sat under a giant oak tree, reading *Tender Buttons* by Gertrude Stein when a swirl of wind caused him to look up from his reading, just in time to see a very attractive young woman chasing her papers across the park. She was wearing Levi's jeans and a white peasant top, holding on to a sun hat that seemed to be flopping all over. In a valiant and his good deed for the day, he got up to help. That was their introduction.

From that day forward, they met at the park every Wednesday and Saturday afternoon, precisely at two. In the beginning, they brought only a blanket to sit on, but as time moved on, she would bring soft drinks and he the snacks. They talked about current events, music, and books, just "getting to know each other" conversation. However, their talks were never about going out on a formal date. This was by his design. Everything they did was about the present time, just two people enjoying each other, the outdoors, and a good discussion.

Months pass and now they begin to bring foodstuff, like breast of chicken sandwiches that he made and her homemade pies. He also brought a bottle of Riesling that they both liked. He brought a poetry book and she her sketching pad, plus a portable radio. Sometimes, they sat without talking, just two people who care about each other, an item as they say, without any commitments. He never asks, and she never commits.

Finally, after eight months of meeting at the park, he decided that they should go out on their first date. "What shall we do?" she asks.

"Well, to tell you the truth, I'm not really sure. Let's go to the movies?" he says.

"Okay, that sounds like fun. What shall we go see?"

"I hear there is a movie called *Midnight Cowboy*. They say it is good."

"Is it a western?"

"Not sure," he answers.

They shared a box of popcorn and pop. They both liked the movie but decided to do more research on future movies. This movie was a bit hardcore for both.

They meet each other's friends for the first time, and everyone thinks they make a great couple. At parties, it is just the two of them and no one else in the room, or so it seemed to them.

However, it is at the park that gives them the most pleasure. Sitting quietly, reading and drawing is their bond.

Once while listening to the radio, "Sister Golden Hair" by America was playing. He looked at her and for the first time realized that she is a remarkable person. He actually cared a great deal but kept his thoughts and emotions to himself.

For his own personal reasons, they never met each other's families. He would tell her he was going to visit his family but never offers an invitation. She seems okay with this arrangement. "Call me when you get back." He does.

One day, during their weekly park meeting, he tells her that he is getting transferred to another city out of state. She stared at him and says nothing. "When are you leaving?" she finally asks.

"I will be gone by the end of the month," he answers.

"So, what does it mean for us?" she asks.

He doesn't answer.

As the weeks go by, they see little of each other. He is busy going back and forth looking for a place to live. When they do hook up, nothing is said…it's just two people trying to cope with the inevitable.

His friends are having a going-away pool party for him. As is his custom, someone else was picking her up at her house (he never wanted to know where she lived) and bought her to the party. They met at the party and had a great time with each other. They dance, he drinks, and nothing is said.

The next morning, he got up and packs his car and drives off. Not a note to say good-bye, nothing, just gone.

Two months pass and she calls him. "Can I come live with you?" she asks.

"No! That is out of the question," he answers. "It's best that you find someone else," he said and hangs up.

It is about this time that his daydreaming stops and is now back at Le Bistro. He begins to listen more intently again. She is in the process of recounting stories. *She seemed happy*, he thinks to himself.

Suddenly, she stops talking and stares at him for a few seconds. "What happened to us?"

"I'm not sure what you are asking," he answers.

"You know us. What happened to us, didn't you care?" she asks.

"Of course, I cared," he answers.

"Why didn't you call or want me to live with you?"

"I wish I had a good answer for you, but I don't."

He looks at his watch and says, "I have to catch flight. It was a thrill seeing you again." He got up and gave her a kiss on the cheek. He walked away.

"Wait! I want to give you my address and cell number in case your business brings you back. Perhaps we can get together."

"Sure, that would be nice." He takes the piece of paper and puts it in his coat pocket. "See you," he says.

A sudden chill brings a tear to her eyes. "See you."

On his way to the airport, "Sister Golden Hair" by America is playing. It's the song that, over all these years, reminds him of her—of the first time they met. Her long blonde hair, the jeans, and peasant shirt. How he missed her every day after he left.

He checks in the rental car and begins to walk toward the concourse to check in his luggage. Before boarding, he takes out the piece of paper—the one with her address and cell number—and throws it in the trash. *It sure was a thrill seeing her again*, he thinks to himself.

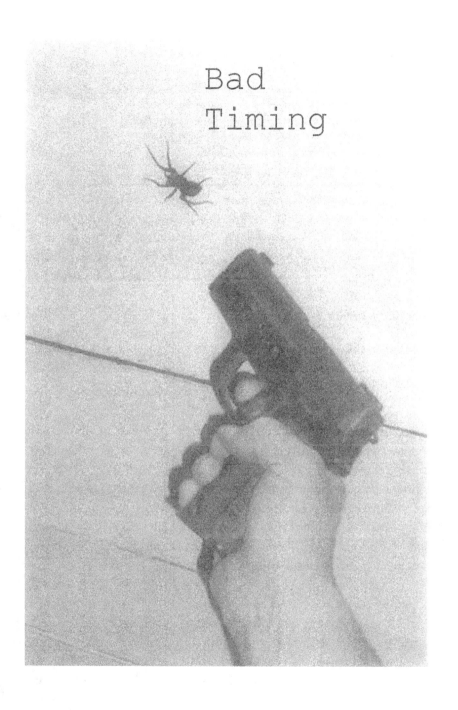

Bad
Timing

Bad Timing

I wasn't caught off guard. I simply had my head turned to the left before someone unexpectedly began yelling at the top of his lungs. "Give me all the money in the register, now!" Like a spinning top, I turned and saw a honey pimple-faced young man—with uncombed, shoulder-length, dishwater blonde hair; Clark Gable ears; ratty beard; blue windbreaker; and wearing mirrored sunglasses—shouting in a high pitch voice, "Give me all the money in the register," all the time pointing a small caliber gun directly at my rib cage.

I could see my appearance in his sunglasses. My droopy face looked whitish; my nostrils narrowing; perspiration droplets forming on my forehead; and my mouth wide open, dry as the Sahara Desert. I was unable to speak or mumble a solitary word. Scared stiff!

Without so much as a trace of panic or worry in his veins, the young robber calmly squeezed the trigger. The gun exploded with a tremendous ear-splitting blast, engulfing every nook in the store, causing the windows to rattle, and producing a throbbing in my ears. I had a fleeting but repulsive scent of gunpowder, then flashes of red, yellow, and blue blinding my eyes momentarily. Then an out-of-body experience caught me looking at the copper bullet spiraling its way toward my body in slow motion. My mind completely froze. I became a petrified statue incapable of moving.

The bullet struck my upper body thrusting me against the wall, knocking over a cigarette stand. Unconsciously, I grabbed my chest. I felt an excruciating pain that flooded throughout my entire body, spitting streams of blood on my hands and clothes, on the floor, and I'm sure the counter. My terror now turned into a feeling of serenity without being excited. No bright white lights, but I began seeing images of family and friends long gone now engulf my mind. I made a great effort to see, but the lights were dimming and the store now entirely covered in a shroud of darkness. No images or sounds, just me hitting the floor, gasping for that last breath of soothing air before I died.

One Final Story

One Final Story

Lance resides in a cheerless, decrepit room above the garage owned by his best friend Jack. Lance is seated at his desk, brandishing long scraggly hair, sporting bright red pajamas, one bare foot and a gray sock on the other. His rickety fingers sleep on the keys of the old Smith-Corona typewriter, ready to strike and launch his overdue and undoubtedly final story.

Lance's desk is located two steps from his bed on the right and two steps from the bathroom on the left. No longer able to walk with the same gait he had in his youth, Lance now shuffles to the bathroom from the bed while holding his bloated stomach to throw up his guts. This is now a daily ritual. Lance, like some drunk sailor who has been in port but a few hours, wobbles back to his desk. Lance is dying from cirrhosis of the liver.

The motionless Lance prays for guidance and inspiration to creep in his mind just one more time before the end. He glares out of the window to watch the early morning sunlight dance in his room, transporting the imageries of a million dust particles swimming through the air, looking for a place to nest.

Forgetting about the story, Lance, with jaundiced eyes and skin, reaches for the near-empty wine bottle that sits on the floor next to an overfilled jar of cigarette butts. "I need one more drink to steady myself," Lance moans. A stretch with unstable hands tips the bottle over, spilling the last drops on the floor. Lance begins to weep as though he has lost his best friend.

Amid rolling tears down his skeletal face, Lance bashes the typewriter keys with anger. His words are a collection of absurd, pathetic, incomprehensible passages with a pointless message that no one understands. Lance curses his lost world of friends who have abandoned him, calling them inept thieves, underhanded backstabbers who aren't fit to be called humans. He doesn't even recognize his own prose, thinking that someone has stolen his manuscript and left him a mess of perplexing text.

Lance vacillates and, for one brief unclouded moment, remembers when they were calling him the next Hemingway; the suave, self-assured, good-looking Lance with the world clamoring for his attention. And why not? His first novel sold millions of copies, and his hungry fellow writers left screaming to wine and dine him. Lance adores every bit of his newfound popularity, especially the drink that instantly rotted his guts.

Nonetheless, Lance continues to torment those around him... with his pompous self-importance. Slipping back to reality, Lance rips open the window and yells at Jack to bring him another bottle. Jack disregards his friend. Jack's soul is devastated, and he can't assemble the strength to see his friend relapse. "One last drink," bellows Lance. Jack jumps in his car and, with screeching tires, drives off to pursue peace and silence, knowing that his friend is progressing down the desolate path of self-destruction.

With concentration and memory expired, Lance creeps back to the desk. Lance, gawking at the Smith-Corona typewriter, his hands shake uncontrollably, fingers positioned on the keys, readies himself to begin typing his story.

With bloodshot eyes, Lance types the title of his book, *The Alcoholic*. All of a sudden, Lance grabs his alcohol-withered chest, foam flowing from his mouth as his spindly body tumbles from the chair. Resting on the floorboards, transgressing eyes gazing at the ceiling, Lance will never finish the story or consume another drink.

The Last Waltz

The Last Waltz

My friend, what makes you think that she, of all the people you have hurt over the years, will ever talk with you again?

After all, wasn't your unceremonious, impertinent, and neurotic behavior that shoved her away in the first place? That you showed little to no emotion other than your customary apathetic personality that some people find distasteful, while others unpretentiously discount your behavior because that's the way you are.

Moreover, that you took the vulnerability that she exhibited and made a mockery, even being cruel which by the way, was never your intent, hitherto you managed, in your indelible way, to demolish the blossoming relationship to the ground. What difference does it make now? Perhaps she misunderstood your intentions, and that it was entirely her fault, and that perhaps you are the victim in this sorted episode of dramatic reality.

However, none of these scenarios fit any of the previous patterns you exhibited when you danced the last waltz.

So what? Why worry? There is a good chance that you will never cross paths again, but if you do, would you acknowledge her presence? Or will you merely shake her extended hand, as a token of good manners, or will you totally express a nothingness and walk past her as though she didn't exist?

Perhaps, all that can be said, my friend, is that you do have comportment and a sense of decorum; therefore, you would incline to kiss her hand, showing no malice, and display the chivalry once prominent in the court of the kings. But then again, knowing you, who knows?

My friend, you must think of your personal health, which by the way has fallen on hard times recently, and that your only hope of getting better is to be left alone. Unaccompanied, in a room void of noise, with the shades drawn, as to not let the sun penetrate your sensitive eyes. Please, my friend, continue to write, because this exercise will in due time heal your spirit and soul. Write page upon page of things that only make sense to you and a few others.

And discards the manifestations that live in your closet and who have only recently danced the last waltz, because of their desire to help you with your demise that lately has crossed your mind more times than you want to admit. Don't cave into their request. They will only laugh as you hang with a belt around your neck.

Yet you make no excuses for your illness, other than to say that's the way it is, and you find yourself telling others not to worry anymore because you don't want the headaches of your distress to become the focal point in any future conversations.

My friend, you must realize that your condescending attitude about people, in general, has to stop! I recognize that you have never been one to mingle with others and that you get quickly bored with at those who can't stimulate your intellectual interest. And I've known that most times you don't feel any remorse or have the necessity to make excuses, or apologize.

Nevertheless, assuming that you do get better, which you will, what are your intentions?

Reset assure, my friend, that your rudeness and self-absorbance will disappear forever as your body heals itself of the poisons that flow in your veins, and with any luck, you will never rear that ugly head again, and perhaps you will be happy once again.

Although, my friend, I'm beginning to doubt your intentions. So, I will ask once again, what are your plans?

My friend, I pray that you come out of this self-induced coma and become a better person. One that will melt her heart once again with the mere mention of your name. And perhaps with every stroke of the pen, your writings will put a smile on her face and bring her a sense of joy that she so much requires.

My friend, I have known you for many years, and I have come to know that your personality dictates how much time you will spend chasing someone. But my concern is, when will you tire and eventually never talk with her again? How much time does she have? Should she start counting the days which, by the way, depends on your energy level, and that is definitely connected with highbrow conversation and not frivolous repartees.

Nonetheless, I hope is that you, my friend for the ages, will find the calmness and friendliness that once characterized your youth. The days when your effervescent smile that once was the envy of others will reappear. Because I have seen you at your best, especially when I saw you holding her tight during the last waltz.

I saw you and her sitting and whispering and for one brief moment, a smile on her face as she held your hand told me that in some strange way she cared. I realized that for that same moment, you might have felt the same way. But I wonder, my friend, how long will you tolerate that lack of stimulation you so much desire in others?

My friend, I feel pity for both of you. But I realize that nothing will ever change with two stubborn minds who both seem to think that each is right and are not willing to compromise.

What does the future hold for you? Someone else in your life?

Will that make you exultant, my friend? When does your life become more serious in nature? When?

Unfortunately, my friend slowly drifted out of my life. I felt hurt that after so many years, we had lost contact, a connection that I thought would last into our old age.

Then by chance, while traveling in Ohio, I spotted my friend sitting in a bar, drinking wine and talking with a young and attractive woman.

"How are you, my friend? It's good to see you."

"Likewise. I would like for you to meet Mary Kay."

The three of us sat, and he and I began talking about the old days. Then, out of nowhere, he asked about her. And I said that I hadn't seen her in years.

"I sure miss her," he said.

We said our good-byes and would never see him again.

Six months later, I ran into her. She was with the girls. I gave her a hug, and we talked. She asked if I had seen him, and I said no.

I remember the two together, and they were a remarkable couple. And if ever there was love lost, it had to be my friend and her. One as stubborn as the other, and sadly, they never finished the last waltz.

Reason

Reason

Each night, before I crawl in bed, I look out at the darkness of the night and see another season drift by, and I wonder, *Wasn't summer last week, and spring the previous week? What's happening to time?* I remember well in my youth when I could lie in bed all day and not have reclusive anxiety about the seasons of the year.

Now my heart is heavy, and I want to see an unruffled world. I want to see the heavens full of stars and flowers glowing in dazzling colors year-round. But I seem to be losing a battle with my aches and pains that seem to be setting the rules for my existence. I don't want to be that cynical old curmudgeon walking around in stained khakis, held up my suspenders, and cursing under my breath. I still want a slice of the young me.

Sometimes, I am more clearheaded than at other times. It's during these periods when I whip out my pencil and write. I write about whatever comes to mind. Some pleasant memories, while others are not so welcoming. Nonetheless, they all got me to this phase in my life.

I remember vividly when I was nineteen and used to read Rod McKuen's poetry to the prostitutes on Myers Street. Poems about love. I remember how they laughed at my attempted Shakespearean oratory and hand articulation; my effort to bring life to each word—to make the words dance and sing off the pages. After finishing my recital, most clapped, while others gave me a comical yet lascivious look.

In most, I could see their solemn expressions, comparable to striking an untouched nerve while making them think about their childhoods when their lives went from bad to worse. And now they find themselves in this deplorable situation that is making them look older than their youthful years. Worn-out, missing the high steps and smiles they once had in their energetic souls.

The ones that at one time offered the world so much potential. My memories of walking past the Del Monte Market, the Legal Tender, and the Maytag store on Congress and Myers; on my way to see the ladies. However, the further I walked, I became saddened to see the once colorful houses with sidewalks made for one person to walk on and the cactus and desert flowers that aligned each house. Homes with baloneys and linen curtains covering ornate windows and doors. The once beautiful dwellings, now destroyed by time and by the women of the night. Women who had no interest in the upkeep of this once vibrant street and only saw the houses as a means to make money.

Alas, I have to move on and bring my book of poetry to other unfortunates...wherever they might be.

It's Friday afternoon, and I sat on a park bench overlooking the city. People happily walking from here to there, and I hoped that urban renewal stays clear and doesn't destroy the vivaciousness like it has in so many other cities.

I saw shoppers carrying bags of all sizes, cheerfully talking about the sales and how much money they saved; all the while trying to decide where to have lunch.

While the impatient jaywalker, causing several drivers to slam on their brakes and the subsequent exchange of expletives, while onlookers take sides on whose fault it was. Minutes later, it's all is over and done, and the anxieties go back to normal.

A woman about thirty, wearing a blue dress that hasn't seen an iron, sat next to me on the bench. Her blue eyes have lost their twinkle, and she has wrinkles on her leathery face. Her voice has a deep raspy sound caused by one of a thousand cigarettes she has inhaled.

She asked me what I have on my lap. I told her that it's a book of poetry.

"Can you read me something?" she asked.

I fumbled through my book entitled *Listen to the Warm* by Rod McKuen, looking for something unique. "I hope you like it," I said.

"Two. Be gentle with me, new love. Treat me tenderly. I need the gentle touch, the soft voice, the candlelight after nine. There've been so many who didn't understand so give me all I see in your timid eyes but give it gently. Please."

When I finished reading, I saw a tear roll down her worn face, and then she said. "I liked it very much, and now I feel good inside." The only time I saw her smile.

"Could you give me money or a cup of coffee?" she asked.

I reached in my pocket and hand her my last dollar.

She got up from the park bench and, without showing any gratitude, walked across the street to the methadone clinic where I'm sure she gets her daily cure from whatever drug has poisoned her body and a place where they offer free coffee and donuts.

I stood and made my way to the dry river bed not far from the city. I walked over the river stone to a place under the wellworn bridge that connects the rich people's dwellings from the city. I lie down to take a nap and use my poetry book as a pillow. I stare at the bird's nest above me, and I wonder if anyone is home. Seconds later, the cool crosswinds cause me to fall into a deep slumber…for the next few hours, I'm able to stop thinking about her or me.

I was lucky to have my time in the city before it was destroyed beyond recognition. But I was even more fortunate to have a brief encounter with the breathtaking women of the night and the drug addict. They were who they were, and I had no right to pass judgment. But then again, I can only wonder how they survived without my book of poems.

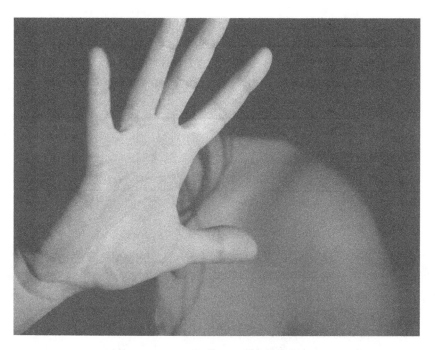

Blank

Blank

We sat in an undescriptive hotel lobby, on a settee, gazing into each other's eyes for what appeared to be a lifetime. I felt this unfettering desire to kiss her, wondering what it would feel like to touch her soft lips. And I saw in her eyes the same passion. My thoughts were so blameless and virtuous that, unbeknownst to me, I loved this woman who was holding my hand with tenderness that seemly came from her heart.

Instead, without saying another word, we got up and went our separate ways. We were gone to be with our friends who never suspected that we could be involved other than just friends. What a cruel world that we had come so far, yet never expressed the truth that two people should share. We didn't take advantage of the moment, a moment that would never happen again. That one particular time and place where nothing mattered, just two people who had a connection, then in one gentle whisper, let it go.

My aching heart was full of angst that I've made a terrible mistake. The spirit that was lying within me was no longer a comfort but now a sorrowful hurt that I will never get over. I've taken a position of *unclarity*, wondering how many times my mind will overtake my sensibility, fostering a deep feeling of regret, that will surely follow me daily until my dying day. I prayed for forgiveness that one day will make me whole again, yet I wonder what was to become of me.

That night, as I drove away, my thoughts drifted from the reality of being who I was to the uncertainty of who I wanted to be, and the truth about seeing her, disappearing with each mile I drove. As much as I tried to turn back, the pain I inflicted could never be undone, not with a bouquet of flowers or letters of apology. Nothing would ever destroy the cruel moment when words would cut deeply into the core of someone's heart and soul. So I continued to drive faster and faster, hoping that in some way, I could outdistance myself from what I had done, knowing that my actions caused her to get up and walk away.

Driving into the darkness of the night, I realized that my intentions, which appeared to be noble at the time, were merely a source of my own personal entertainment. This was a mean of purging myself of people who cared about me, for I never wanted closeness or to be touched by anyone. I wanted solitude to pick and choose whatever or whoever as my desires dictated without apology. However, I found myself for the first time wanting another chance, perhaps just to be friends or worse to satisfy my ego, which I guarded as carefully as I do my bible.

My all-night driving had taken me to the outskirts of a town that I didn't recognize. Perhaps it was an omen, telling me that I was a lost soul who should seek redemption. Or that I should go back and face the realities of my actions and seek forgiveness that I was quite certain will never happen. Nonetheless, I was where I was because of me and no one else. There was no going back. I must face the reality that nothing was going to change with me or anyone else, lest they apostasy.

It was daybreak, and I decided to pick up a hitchhiker who was carrying a guitar. He was younger than me with a scraggly beard, long unwashed hair, clothes that haven't been washed in months, and that smell deplorable. Other than where he was going, there was little conversation, but that was all right because it distracted me from the woman who I will never see again. I drove eastward into the glaring sun. Three hours later, I pulled into a truck stop where my companion bid me a farewell as he jumped into a semitruck that was headed north.

I gassed up and walked into the restaurant where I promptly see her, sitting in every booth, tempting me to sit with each and offer another apology that will go unheeded. Could I be so wicked that guilt was following from one place to another? When do I get absolution? When does it end? I decided to take a seat at the counter and order a cup of coffee. Perhaps the hot brew will clear my mind. Perhaps I just needed to sleep.

A petite young woman, wearing a baseball cap that was hiding her blond hair, sat next to me. I turned to give her a polite smile, and I was captivated by her blue eyes. We struck up a conversation, and she told me that she was headed to Texas, Wichita Falls to be precise. She went on to say that she was leaving Long Beach after getting out of an awful marriage and was taking a nursing job at the military hospital. Then she asked me for direction, and I told her that there was approximately eight or more hours of road time, but she was more than welcomed to stay at my house. With a slight disinclination, she accepted my offer and followed me to my home.

Finally, I was beginning to feel somewhat happy and thought of the one I left, what seems like years ago, slowly crept out of my mind. I turn on the radio and listened to "I Can Understand It," and the shadow of my sins came flowing back, making me sad all over again. That I could be in love with her was mind-altering, and yet I felt myself wondering, what if? There was no truth other than to say that I was dejected. I felt myself in a pitiful state, wondering if I will ever recover as a whole person. Perhaps the social being that I was will disappear in sadness and fall prey to the grief that was lying inside my heartbroken body. What was left in my life except the changing of the seasons? I feared that my gloom will never see the beauty of the rain falling over the flora, or of the snowfall, and that I shall never feel the gentle summer breeze made worse by the thought of not ever seeing her again regardless of the time of the year.

We arrived in my house, and like the well-mannered compere that I was, I told her to make herself at home. I turned on the, prepared a plate of canapes, and poured her a glass of wine that she appeared to appreciate.

She seemed to be impressed by my kindness and etiquette. Perhaps this was the first time in her young life that a man can be so caring to a total stranger, unlike her ex-husband, who continuously berated her. I took off her shoes and fluffed up the sofa pillows so that she might relax. I excused myself, walked to the bedroom, and put clean sheets on the bed and fresh towels in the bathroom. I laid out a bathrobe for such circumstances. I went back to the living room and sat next to her. I asked about her family, her likes, and dislikes, all the while thinking about someone else.

I leaned in and kissed her, and she reciprocated without vanity. We went into the bedroom and made tender and passionate love until we fell asleep. The next morning, feeling better than I had in days, I got up to find her gone. She left a note with her new address and telephone number, which I promptly threw away. It was beautiful, but I didn't demand any tenderness or any affection that I couldn't repay. From time to time, I thought about the nurse, but like everything in my life, it slowly disappeared.

Months had gone by, and I thought less and less of the one who I couldn't have a meaningful relationship, and I feared that I would never see her again. I suppose the impression she made on me will always be there, but I felt sure that she will never disappear from my thoughts even if I tried. For one brief moment, the stars in the heavens aligned, but two foolish people couldn't take advantage of the opportunity. One was scared to have a friendly relation, and the other was too involved in his own world, afraid of nothing except his own ghost.

I saw myself in the mirror with swollen eyes full of grief. My body was withering from the inside out. I no longer yearn for the company of woman who, over the years, have brought me so much joy. Now there was only an empty space. I was hoping that she will secretly come back. There was so much I needed to say to her now, if only she was just standing here, but what were the odds?

Today, I got word through a mutual friend that she married another, and for a split second, hitherto lasting a lifetime. I felt a pain in my heart. However, I understood that everything worked out for the best. I screwed up, and perhaps it was my lot to spend the rest of my years, regretting my every move.

Perhaps if I had listened to my heart and been truthful from the beginning, I might find myself in a better situation than feeling grief-stricken, or better yet, if I could have seen the words and spoke from the heart instead of spewing harsh words that sealed my faith. Without her, how could I exist? She made me feel better about myself although she never knew. I've lost at love before, and somehow, I managed to survive. This too will pass, and tomorrow, I will suffer the anguish once more, this time alone.

Late last night, feeling so lonely that I couldn't sleep. I went looking for her, she and only she, and not some undesirable, who in the past would be an acceptable company. I needed her in that instant. I was walking sadly, thinking about how she looked the last time I saw her. My grief was now pouring down my face. I asked myself if I will ever get a second chance. I was dreaming that by some miracle, she would land before my feet. And what would I do then? Perhaps I would take her in my arms and kiss her with such passion that she would never leave me again.

But how could I feel this way when I didn't even know her name? Or perhaps if I had never met her, would my existence be different? Would I be more contented in my life? Furthermore, could I have composed this narrative about her?

The Twentieth Day of July

The Twentieth Day of July

The day is as pure and clean as newly washed sheets. Innocent traces of gentle northerly winds encircle the crib where the infant lies. His eyes closed tightly with an angelic smirk on his face, as those keeping a secret from his mother.

His mother, with delicate skin and soft red hair, sits on a wicker chair on a porch opposite main street, exposing her uncovered breast, while reading the latest copy of *Glamour* magazine, wishing that she could get her figure back, just like the models in the glossy magazine and longing for a pair of nylon stockings.

Numerous couples walk by her gloomy rental house and see nothing but a shameful, undesirable, and unfit mother, who sits gingerly exposing herself in public like some harlot.

Whereas their fervent husbands, unable to contain the energy that drifts from their eyes to other parts of their bodies, don't mind the view a bit, even encouraging their hefty wives to take a daily stroll by the young motherhouse under the pretense of getting much-needed exercise.

The young mother, unaffected by her surroundings or her appearance, glances at each passerby and simply smiles. A sad smile because of the disheartening envy of not having her husband to walk with her and the baby—a baby that her husband doesn't know exists.

How could he? They only met twelve months earlier at the town roadhouse that she unashamedly patronized after work. With merely a few drinks that connected them, they married within the week.

Now he's gone to fight some in some war that she doesn't comprehend. Yet, she keeps her ear to the radio for the latest news. Everything made worse because he hasn't written since he left two months past.

Nonetheless, as large as any pregnant women could get, she worked at the drugstore until two days before she gave birth to a baby boy—a boy who doesn't resemble anybody but an old man with sparse black hair and who sleeps content, unaware of his ambiance.

Still, with all the hardship, she managed to save six dollars and twenty-five cents from her weekly paycheck of the twenty dollars after taxes to pay the house rent.

Necessity is driving her back to work, and now she must consider daycare for the infant. She makes inquiries but quickly realizes the high cost of daycare is beyond her means.

She runs an advertisement in the local newspaper, requesting a babysitter, and has many applicants but no one wants to work for the seventy-five cents a day she is willing to pay. Downhearted, she doesn't know what to do until a knock on the door.

There at the screen door stands a young nappy-haired, simple-looking black woman of about eighteen—wearing a yellow cotton dress, a belt that doesn't hold the old dress together, and threadbare shoes—asking if the job has been filled.

The young mother, holding the baby tightly in her arms, says no and invites the young black woman into the house.

"Please take a seat. Would you like something to drink?"

"No, ma'am, I'm doin' good. That, sure enough, is a pretty-lookin' little girl."

"It's a boy. His name is Samuel."

"Samuel, like in the Bible?" asks the young black woman.

"Oh, I suppose. I just thought it was a pretty name."

"Have you ever taken care of a baby before? By the way, what is your name?"

"My mama, she calls me Emma Lou. And yes, ma'am, I have six little brother and sisters dat I looked after. Mama, she has to work two jobs, and there was no one else to exceptin' me. But now she has a new boyfriend, and there ain't no room for me. So she told me, I gotta be moving along."

And so, the women talk for over an hour; Emma Lou, even holding baby Samuel, who is sound asleep, and wakes only when he's hungry or in need of changing of the putrid-smelling diaper.

There is an instant bond between the women, and soon, Samuel's mother offer Emma Lou the job that Emma Lou eagerly accepts.

"Where do you live?"

"Well, ma'am, I kinda been sleepin' on a bench at the bus station. 'Til I'm told to move on by that big fat policeman."

"Go and get your things. You can live here if you want."

"This all I got. I ain't got no belongings."

"You don't have other clothes?"

"No, ma'am!"

Emma Lou moves in and is quickly given a blue rayon dress, undergarments, a winter coat, and a pair of sturdy low heels shoes. A bit worn, but for Emma Lou, these are the first new clothes she has ever owned.

As time goes on, not only does Emma Lou take care of baby Samuel, but she also keeps the house clean, washes the dirty diapers, and cooks. At the end of each month, Emma Lou mails her mama twenty dollars and saves two dollars and fifty cents for herself.

Most of the townspeople are in an uproar because a colored woman as moved in with the white woman and is taking care of a white bastard child. No one believes that she is married to a soldier.

Two of the nastiest women in town have the audacity to go to the pharmacy and demand that the owner fires the unfit mother.

"I'll talk with her tomorrow," answers the pharmacy owner, but he never does.

An entire year goes by and no word from her husband. Distraught, she cries nightly while cradling Samuel, who is now crawling and making significant efforts to walk.

Emma Lou listens from her bedroom, but there is nothing she can do. She gets out of bed, kneels and prays hard that little Samuel's mama's husband comes home soon.

Each day, she checks the mailbox, but there is no letter from her husband. She goes to the army recruiting office to seek information on her husband, but the officers on duty haven't been able to find his whereabouts. The commanding officer has even suggested that perhaps he is using another name.

"Are you sure that's his name?"

She shows him a copy of the marriage license. The officer glances at the piece of paper with the names of Maggie Jones and Jack Bruce; he makes a few notes on his pad, then hands the certificate back to Maggie.

"I'll keep looking, miss."

"It's mis'ess. Thank you."

Maggie walks out the office wiping away tears, wondering what to do next. She walks back to the pharmacy and is met at the door by the owner, who tells her that he has to let her go.

"I'm sorry, Maggie, but business is slow. You understand?"

"But I have a baby to take care of what I am supposed to do?"

Maggie's world, in one day, has gone from bad to worse. She buys a newspaper, goes to the park, and sits on a bench, then quickly goes through the want ads. She observes numerous jobs but understands that no one will hire her. She has heard all the gossip about the black girl and the bastard child.

The freshness of the night is gone as she walks home. She walks up to the porch and sits in the wicker chair, staring at nothing, discerning roughly everything.

Emma Lou arranges Samuel in the crib and walks outside. "What's troublin' you, Missy?"

"Well, Emma, I've lost my job, and I'm sure what to do, and I won't be able to pay you," says the panic-stricken woman.

"Don't you worry none. I'm stayin' and look ova little Samuel."

Maggie grabs Emma Lou and gives her a big hug.

Winter is rapidly approaching, and there is still no prospect of a job. Her savings are running low, and she only has one more month of rent money and food, except for Samuel is rationed between the woman.

At night, they all sleep in the same bed to keep warm. In the mornings, they layer on clothes and stay in the bedroom where it is warmer.

They have put sheets around the window seal and under the door to keep the wind out and only go to the kitchen to grab biscuits and water.

The landlord has been around asking for rent money, although they still have thirty days before the rent is due. He's an unkind man, who walks with a pretentious limp that kept him out of the army. His wife is more considerate and urges her husband to be more understanding of the woman.

Desperate, she acquires a job at the Nob Hill Burlesque. Nob Hill is a semi-grungy bar located on the outskirts of town. The cowshed-looking saloon is typically jam-packed with the regular boozers, drug pushers, blue and white-collar men who weren't drafted and looking for a good time before having to face the little woman and kids at home. There's also a collection of single and married women trying to break into the striptease business.

After a few tunes by the house band and a standup comedy show by Jackie the Joke man, it's time for Heat Wave as she prefers to be known when on stage.

On her first night, she wears a gold mask, long fake diamond earrings, sheer black dress, and black stilettoes. Clothes that she borrowed from the other girls.

The band begins playing "Harlem Nocturne," and Heat Wave starts seductive gyrating her hips. Midway through her performance, she begins to unpeel her clothes one piece at a time.

The boisterous crowd goes wild with their uncontainable shouting to "take it off," "take it off," hollering that resonates throughout the smoke-filled bar. Some of the more inebriated men even try to leap onto stage to get a touch of Heat Wave. Coins and dollar bills tossed onto the stage. The entire bar goes into a frenzy, an uproar as the drunks shout for more. Meanwhile, Heat Wave finishes her set and begins to pick up her night salary off the dance floor.

After she fills her purse with the money, she sits at the bar to have one quick drink before heading home and where she will sleep until noon.

The next day, she sits on the bed, counting her money, when suddenly, Samuel jumps onto the bed, and the two begin playing. First, by bouncing on the worn mattress and then having a pillow fight. The thought of money is forgotten; Samuel comes first.

After two hours of roughhousing, she, Emma, and Samuel sit down for lunch of soup and crackers.

"How was it, Missy? asks Emma.

"It was horrible!" She says no more.

After lunch, she goes back to count her money. She separates the coins by denomination and the same for the dollar bills. The total is fifteen dollars and fifty-six cents. She is ecstatic.

"Emma, get Samuel dressed. The three of us are going out to buy a few groceries, and on the way home, we will stop at the soda shop and buy triple decker ice cream cones." It gives her time to get home and changed for her shift at Nob Hill.

That evening, while she walks to Nob Hill, she can't stop thinking about how degrading it is for her to undress in front of total strangers, but she can justify on the other hand the money is good.

She works at Nob Hill six days a week for one year, and each night is as bad as the next. The wear and tear on her body are taking its toll, not to mention the several times she was followed home by drunks who robbed and beat her savagely.

One morning, she was found by the mailman, as she lay in a ditch; her clothes torn off, not half a block from her home.

Also, there is constant harassment from the police who like nothing better than picking her up as she walks home at two in the morning, then throwing her in the back seat and raping her and, for good measure, taking her money. Who is she going to tell?

It's challenging to be seductive when she is so tired. Exhausted and bruised, and unusually drained by the degenerates who frequent the bar. Her only saving grace is that she has managed to accumulate two thousand dollars.

During this same period, she is now paying Emma Lou one dollar a day. She is excited with her newfound wealth and is now saving every penny, although she occasionally buys Samuel a toy. She has even quit sending her greedy mother money. Her worldly funds are almost one hundred dollars that she keeps hidden in her mattress.

One evening, before going off to Nob Hill, she tells Emma Lou that she is thinking about quitting her job and buying a small farm on the outskirts of town.

"What do you think, Emma? We can have our own room, and we can grow a nice garden, and we won't be beholding to anyone."

"I think that is a wonderful idea, Missy. But you sure you wants me to go live with you?"

"Emma Lou, you are part of this family. Little Samuel looks at you as his big sister. So you have to come. Also, understand it will be hard work, and because I won't have a job, I won't be able to pay you. That is, until we can sell vegetables from your garden."

"Oh, Missy, this sure is exciting news."

She works for six more months. Putting up with all the aggravation a single person can endure and saving every penny that falls on the dance floor.

On the twentieth day of July, which is also Samuel's birthday, she says good-bye to Nob Hill forever.

The following week, she buys a farmhouse on five acres of land. The house was built in 1922, but the owners fell on hard times and had to vacate the property.

She spends fifteen hundred dollars on a derelict white house with a green roof. Inside the farmhouse, there is a living room, kitchen, dinette, one bath, and two bedrooms. It also has a porch with missing planks; worse is five acres of weeds.

Inside the house, paint is beginning to peel from the living room walls, and there are cobwebs in every part of the house, even the occasional snake come slithering from holes in the walls.

There is some furniture in the house. A dust-covered gold velvet sofa and matching chair, an oval braided rug with touches of brown, mustard, blue, red, and orange. Wood table and two chairs in the dinette, a wood-burning stove in the kitchen, wood vanity with a round mirror in the larger of the two bedrooms. Each bedroom has bedframes in need of mattresses, and the entire house in dire need of burnishing.

The women, eagerly begin scrubbing the house, while Samuel sits on the floor, occupying himself with a spider. His mother watches Samuel closely with a smile, realizing that her boy is learning about the world.

Even four of the girls from Nob Hill have come to help. They have pitched in and purchased two mattresses, kitchen utensils, and plates. In the evenings, the four women wash and go back to Nob Hill to start their jobs as strippers.

Two weeks go by and the house is beginning to look presentable. She and Emma Lou are tired and decide they should take a break and walk two miles into town to buy an ice cream cone. The three are excited with the day off but more eager for the ice cream cone.

The next day, she walks into town to buy a few groceries, then stops at the feed store to see how much chickens cost. At the feed store, she is greeted by the owner, Bob Jones, whom she recognizes from Nob Hill.

"How much are the chicks?"

"For you, honey, I think free would be a good price. How about a drink tonight?" says the repugnant Bob.

"No, thanks. I'll make due."

"Ah, come on. There no need to be that way."

"What if I tell your wife about the proposition, Bob? Perhaps, she won't be so understanding about your comments."

"Get out of here, you whore."

With groceries in hand, she walks back to her farm and sits at the dining table and puts her hands on her head, wondering how she, Samuel, and Emma Lou will survive and wonders if the previous family had the same problems.

The next day, while inspecting the five acres of weeds, she notices a handle of something entrenched in the ground. It takes several hours to ultimately unearth the object and discovers in an old ploy. Perhaps left by the man who tried but failed at growing anything on this hard and rocky ground. Nonetheless, she digs it out, then spends several more hours to get it clean.

It's a push ploy, but it doesn't matter. The next morning, Maggie and Emma Lou begin the difficult job of trying to clear at least a portion of this strong-featured land. Without gloves, the woman quickly begins forming blisters, their legs hurting an indescribable pain, their backs and shoulders aching. At noon, they have lunch and go to bed sore and worn out. Tomorrow is another day.

On day two, they slow down, even taking time to play with Samuel, whose only toys lately are the rocks his mother and Emma Lou have cleared from the unbreakable field. The women decide to wrap their hands with towels as their makeshift gloves. They work until dark.

On day three, dark rainclouds begin developing south of the county, and before long, the deluge starts pouring down in buckets. This is a much-needed rain for the region and especially for the millpond the women didn't know existed in the hindmost part of the five acres. Water that they will need to irrigate once the vegetables are planted. It gives the women time to recuperate before they tackle the land again.

They have also found that the roof has numerous leaks, so the woman place buckets to catch the rain, then empty the containers in a rain barrel on the side of the house. Holes in the roof, another unexpected surprise. More out-of-pocket expenses, and the field is still not unfinished.

Months go by and, slowly, the progress in the fields become noticeable. The women begin hauling the rocks to the pond with the idea of building a retaining wall, then set up some type of irrigation system.

Emma Lou begins to pick up a boulder, and unbeknownst to her, a large rattlesnake is lying in wait. The poisonous snake strikes Emma Lou on the forearm, and Emma Lou lets out a bloodcurdling cry. Maggie hears the scream and goes to aid and finds Emma Lou passed out.

Maggie can see the snake slither off and immediately knows that this is a life-threatening situation. She ties a tourniquet around Emma Lou's arm, picks her up, and rushes two miles into town, yelling for help. Maggie finally makes into to town and finds a doctor's office but is too late. Emma Lou is dead.

With no money for a proper funeral, Maggie and her strip joint friends have Emma Lou buried in a piece of the farmland. They manage to solicit an alcoholic, ex-communicated minister, who is a frequent visitor to Nob Hill, to say a few words over their beloved Emma Lou. He only charges the women a bottle of rye.

Late into the evening, the women stay to comfort Maggie. Jointly, they ask Maggie to give up the farming notion and relocate back to town. They tell her that Nob Hill isn't so bad, and she can still make good money.

Maggie, thanks each but says that she is more determined than ever and will stay for Samuel and Emma Lou.

For two months, Maggie mourns the loss of her friend, while Samuel continues to be inconsolable to the death, not fully understanding what it all means.

While Maggie spends time clearing the field, Samuel pulls wild flowers daily and takes them to Emma Lou's grave. He sits on a stone and cries uncontrollably, asking her to come back. Maggie watches her son grow up from a distance.

Three years have come and gone, and Maggie is now growing corn, an assortment of vegetables, and watermelons. She even has chickens and beehives.

She has even built a produce stand in front of her house, where she sells everything she has grown, including fresh eggs and jars of honey. Maggie is not wealthy by any means but has enough business from the townspeople, who have forgotten Nob Hill and is respected as a good businesswoman.

Samuel has started school, and every morning, precisely at seven, there is a big yellow bus that picks him up and carries him to school, where the shy boy is making friends.

On a warm afternoon, as Maggie takes a break from the produce stand and sits on the porch step, she notices a man walking on the road. The man looks tired, his clothes worn, and doesn't seem to have a suitcase. Maggie figures that he is transient.

But as he gets closer, Maggie seems to know the man.

The man, with yesterday's growth, stands by the fence and says, "Hi, Maggie."

Maggie looks bewildered and doesn't know what to say.

"Hi, Maggie. Don't you recognize me? It's Jack, Jack Bruce."

Disoriented, Maggie just looks, trying to figure what to say. "Jack, I thought you were off fighting in the war. Where have you been? Why haven't you written? I spent years wondering what had happened to you. Where have you been, Jack Bruce?"

Maggie begins to cry, inconsolably.

"Well, Maggie, I have been in prison and just got out two weeks ago. I wrote, but I was too ashamed to mail the letters, humiliated that you would know I was no good."

"Are you hungry?"

"Yes, I am."

"Well, come into the house, and I will fix you a tomato sandwich and some ice tea."

Without hesitation, Jack Bruce enters the house and waits for his sandwich. As Maggie prepares lunch, she also tells Jack about Samuel, who is now five years old.

Jack is excited beyond description and wants to know everything about the little boy. But Maggie quickly quashes Jack's ideas and puts him in his place.

"He's a good little boy, and you aren't allowed to come into this house and try to take over his life. I won't allow it! Is that understood? Also, if you stay, you will sleep in the spare bedroom, and you will work in the field."

In the days to come, Samuel is confused and doesn't understand that Mr. Bruce, as he calls him, is actually his father. So, Samuel keeps more to himself, afraid to play or interact with Mr. Bruce. He begins to gravitate closer to his mother, who herself has become more protective.

At night, Maggie watches her husband undress, and for an instant, she wants him in her bed. The temptations that linger for any normal woman are there—in the other room. Maggie wants to be held, to have strong hold her tightly and comfort her, and especially a warm body at nights. But something in her gut tells her to keep Jack at a distance. On the other hand, perhaps she is too hard on Jack.

Jack Bruce is an easygoing sort of guy. He is tall, with muscles earned while working on the chain gang in prison. He has dark wavy hair with light eyes that are an instant magnet to all the woman in town and who envy Maggie, although they are not entirely certain of the living arrangements at the farmhouse.

In the evenings, Jack wants Maggie to get a babysitter, so they can go into town and dance. But Maggie is tired and would rather spend time with Samuel, working on his homework.

"Come on, Maggie. You gotta get out of place from time to time. Old Samuel there is smart enough, you don't have to help him with homework every night."

"Here's five dollars, Jack. Why don't you go to the bowling alley and have some beers with you friends?"

"All right, honey."

"I'm not your honey," answers Maggie.

The following day, Maggie walks Samuel to the bus stop, then notices that Jack is not in the fields. She walks into his room and finds an unslept bed. A panic crosses her chest. She wonders if perhaps Jack had an accident. She pours a cup of coffee and sits, wondering and worried.

An hour later, Jack comes stumbling into the kitchen. His shirt is torn and bloody.

"Jack, what happened?"

"Oh, I had a fight with some of the boys. It was nothing."

"Where have you been?"

"Well, I kinda stayed at Angie's house."

"What in the hell do you mean?"

"It was nothin'."

Whatever hope there was for Jack has slowly gone down the drain. It is now becoming difficult for Maggie to have him around. The little bit of trust is gone, and for Jack, it doesn't matter. He works on the farm like a slave help, while drawing a meager salary. The only upside is having a roof over his head and meals twice a day.

On a bright sunny afternoon, Jack is out in the field pulling corn from the stocks. He puts the corn in a bag and drags it to the stand. He takes a drink of water, dons his hat, and begins walking down the dirt road, never to return.

Maggie watches him from the kitchen and begins to weep. She wants to go after him but resist the temptation. Little Samuel comes running from outside and wants to know where his daddy is going. It's too late for all.

The time has passed quickly. Samuel is getting ready to graduate from high school and then join the army. Maggie's business is now profitable, and now has enough money to hire a full-time helper, and Jack Bruce was killed trying to hop a train on the twentieth day of July.

Exhale

Exhale

It was clearly an impossibility to distinguish the truth from the two who exposed themselves to be righteous and those who professed to be on the right hand of God when each had more blemishes than the canonized saints. And yet one can chastise the other for their insincerity and cruelness while the other, unable to support their position, simply concealed in humiliation. That once, they could acknowledge a fondness for the other, since childhood, now had abandoned the notion of friendship and that one opted for words that pierced deeply and destroyed the soul of the one without vicious malice.

Deep into the night, the degraded one contemplated the reshaping of the lost relationship while the other slept without a care in the world, an acknowledgement of the virtuous self without culpability.

There once was a time when a neighbor spoke to the neighbor, and there existed clean air, along with vibrant mind. As the days grew longer, there appeared no signs of a moon that everyone once admired, now only a sad song that was rarely played.

Forgive their immaturity and their useless pursuit of the truth that neither wanted to admit but existed like the sparrow and the dove. And the flight of the seagull without fear nevertheless knew that sudden death will claim its life should it venture too far into the sky, a slow death that will tear apart its wings and cast it forever into the sea.

Why continue with this fruitless pursuance that subsist only in the intellectual mind? But this wasn't unfeigned with lies in the soul that wasn't a soul and absolutely without a doubt was unaffected by the rain that rolled down his cheek. Unable to move, paralyzed with angst and the sorrow that came only in winter.

His movement from day-to-day is nonexistent, while his body floating in a sea of disappointment that once strikes where the snake can't reach. He devoured the nourishment with sadness that made him weak, yet again angry that he had fallen prey to the viciousness of the vile serpent. His mind, not his mind, wanting recompense for his forthright knowledge of the nothingness that searches for the truth.

And she, lonely and vulnerable, hitherto incapable of admitting that in some peculiar way she admired this eccentric man, who was astonishingly unpretentious in his conduct, nonetheless conjugal like so many that she had come across.

Forgive the two, for they waited for perfection that didn't exist and will never be found in others. She simply didn't care and will remain lonely until the end; and he, neurotic from the up evil that was his life, will subsist lengthier than all others and expire a recluse expecting her return.

And the world will continue, less the two who squandered precious minutes waiting and craving more time with each other but couldn't because of selfish pride that ate away at their hearts.

Bring the curtain down and let the woman who looked eager to please but in some way thinking about the realities of life, while he, with more imagination than soul, devoured every word, less those imaginary walls that trickled in and out of the minds of the one who was lost.

He lolled on the beach and was half asleep while the sun darkened his already dark skin. Then the salty air and the palm trees swaying, casted a silhouette on the letter writer who declared perpetuity so eloquently that it went unfazed.

And she continued in a stubborn fashion, unfazed, and having set the rules, thought that the control was hers, yet sitting close to the phone, waiting for a call that surely will never come. And after her appearance was gone, she pondered what happened to the man who once displayed attentiveness.

Silence was the wind that transported sorrow from one hamlet to the other while the two tenants paid little courtesy to message of forgiveness because somewhere in the middle lay the truth.

The Christian souls who neither understood nor appreciated the commandment, "Thou shall not kill," while breathing Christianity every Sunday yet with a lack of understanding that every vile word spoken would kill the spirit of the other.

About Last Night

About Last Night

As is my custom when traveling, I prefer staying in hotels that are close to parks and restaurants. I do this for the sole purpose of not taking away from my passion for running and from the dislike of having to hunt for a suitable restaurant which in itself can be a major headache. I require some order in my life.

In fact, lately, I've had to be extremely efficient with my time. Yet, it seems that I can't say no, and so I find myself with an excessive amount of work. Various projects all with due dates that appear unrealistic to meet.

I got myself corralled into to doing the nearly impossible, that is leaving little to no time for a personal life. Especially having quality time with the little woman. Not that we are social animals, but the one at home needs a break, even if it's a burger from McDonald's.

The grind of the numerous projects is taking more than forty-hours work per week. And I realize that no one promised me regular hours, but for all practical purposes, my time is no longer mine to control. My existence is measured by results, which leaves me little time for anyone. The one at home understands my passion for succeeding and is willing to let me pursue my ambitions, but I find myself becoming more and more selfish.

I prepare for another high priority trip. I am unable to book reservations at my regular hotel, which has resulted in securing the only room available, which is situated in the heart of the city. I don't have an aversion for downtown, but it's not my preference. I don't like the dreary feeling you get when all the lights in the skyscrapers are on, but the streets are void of people, and more importantly, my running is made more difficult and unsafe. The children of the night are out in full force and to encounter these individuals is a bit scary, you never know what to expect.

So, I'm stuck in this unobjectionable but lonely hotel. And I know that after my run, I'll be dining from a less than appealing buffet and drinking house wine that I'm sure will have a yesterday production date. I've also become somewhat of snob.

Of course, the dining room is practically empty, and the body count, including me, is six, all of us businessmen, and all of us eating a less than a desirable meal. After my tasteless dinner, I amble to the lounge where an old-timer is wearing a neatly pressed tuxedo, and is playing semi-recognizable tunes on a dusty piano that has seen better days. The total count in the bar is ten. Six of us from the dining room, and four others who stumbled off the naked streets, and who already have a head-start in the drinking department. When the piano player takes his well-deserved break, the room becomes still. It seems that all anyone wants to do is drink.

I don't remember what I had to drink that night. But whatever I had it was more than one. What I do remember is meeting a long-legged blond, with blue bedroom eyes, and a come-hither smile that melted me to the core. She was dressed to the nine's but unpretentious. It was one of those unexpected surprises that happens to some and not to others. Kindred spirits destined for this particular time and place.

She sat next to me at the end of the bar. Instantly, I asked if I could buy her a drink.

"I'll take a frozen Margarita," she said.

"Barkeep, please bring the lady a frozen Margarita, and I'll have a bud."

"Sure pal, coming right up."

We talked well into the night, mostly about me, and it appeared that I was hungry for conversation. The relaxing colloquy prompted me to ask if we could continue our discourse in room #320.

Although it wasn't solely anyone's fault, as adults, we each had the opportunity to say no, and we didn't. Instead, we caved in to a world of unbridled lust. We went into this blunder as though each, especially me, were unattached. Me, with no responsibilities but to the one who waited at home.

I had forgotten about the months of courtship. The battle to win her heart that seemed to take a lifetime. But finally, the one at home irrevocably conceding to my persistence, and to my charm and the promises to be the best I could be and forsaking all others. While at this very moment, she sat at home doing whatever she does, I venture with no conscious into a world of no return.

The heart-melting blond has a child. I believe, she said, a boy. I didn't ask any questions, she just volunteered the information as though it would make a difference. In the first place, it was none of my business, and to be quite truthful, I didn't care. I didn't want to hear her life story or know her name. I wanted nothing that could and would add more guilt, and potentially could affect my performance. That could have an adverse effect on my manhood.

Nonetheless, we continued our nefarious expedition, our exploring, touching each other with a tenderness that I hadn't felt in quite a few years. A sadness streaked across my mind, not for me but the one who waited at home. Unaware, that I had crossed the line that I swore I would never do. So much for promises.

Heated passion lasting for hours and never a word between us. We only paused for a relaxing cigarette and to cool the lips with a drink of water. Bedspread, sheets, pillows laying in every direction of the room made by two uncontrollable sex-hungry, ravenous animals. I never thought of myself other than a normal man with normal desires, but this was akin to exploring myself when I was thirteen or fourteen, when every ten seconds I was thinking about sex. Yet here I was clinking for dear life, hoping with all my uninvited desire for more. To taste the forbidden fruit forever, or at least once more, while being lost and consumed in my own selfish world.

The once self-absorbed and semi-religious me could never be tempted by outside distractions, but I caved in like a kid eating his first candy bar. And in one single moment, I was instantly swept into a world of mortal sin. I stooped so low that I made a mockery of my confessions to the parish priest whose job it was to absolve me of my sins, for that I might become a better person instead of a blight on the institution of religion.

How could I face my mother who drilled the goodness of the cross and the consequences, should I ever cross the line and jump into the fires of hell. Eternal damnation because of a desire I couldn't or wouldn't resist. Living with my paramour in the bottomless pit of hell, enjoying nothing, not even her soft skin and lips. Engulfed in flames with friends, screaming with blistered skin, begging for forgiveness to no one listening.

I suppose my buddies might think of me as somewhat of a hero, wishing they could do what I did, but too afraid to risk everything. To avoid the consequences of losing family and friends, and any monetary gains they might have made while toiling at jobs they didn't care anything about all for just five minutes of ecstasy. Nonetheless, I'm a hero to worship, but also someone to gossip about to their wives, promising the little woman to be at home for dinner every night for the rest of their henpecked life's.

Our minds and body reveling when we climaxed in unison when we expended that last gasp, and relaxing for a moment that we could give our worn out, sweltered bodies, an opportunity to revive with less than five minutes of sleep. But who can sleep when the energy level of our hearts were still beating at near capacity?

So, there I was, calling for room service and ordering anything that would keep us from dehydrating or starving. I thought that perhaps she would just get dressed and leave. But I never envisioned sitting across the table from her eating breakfast, like a couple...an unmarried couple.

I'm not looking my usually dapper self; instead, my hair is a mess, my (our) secretion smeared all over the sheets, and me with morning breath, and the visits to the bathroom, where my natural but embarrassing sounds, unheard except by the one at home. All my disgusting habits in full view, and she still looking as perky as she did last night.

What does one talk about after the carnal experiences of last night and early this morning? Is it mindless small talk while biting down on my English muffin, trying to show the manners my mother taught me years ago? Do I confess to her that this is my first taste of the sinful fruit and would be my last? While I sob like a little girl who lost a toy or do I find the courage and act like an old professional at this sordid, inexcusable behavior? What's the protocol? It's one thing to read all the details in magazines but the reality is much different. The magazine articles are probably written by some pimple-faced neophyte whose only sexual experience comes from the puppet on his right or left hand.

The first time I had sex with the opposite sex was in high school, a week before my seventeenth birthday. I was walking home after school, and a girlfriend of mine called out. She was with a girl I had never seen before, and I didn't realize at the time that this meeting was no coincidence. It was an introduction that unbeknownst to me, would lead to my first romp in the hay. I was as prepared as any guy who thinks that their only worry is condoms, supplied by the well-meaning drug store owner. However, no one tells you how to use them. There isn't a booklet of introduction, it's trial and error... mostly error.

The scene goes as followed: I'm getting worked up with the usual amount of petting, about two minutes, then trying with all my wits to tear open and slip on this flat piece of so-call lubricated rubber. I wasn't very mechanical or good at puzzles, so this piece of rubber was winning the battle. I began to lose the urge, my manhood shrinking, the whole situation becoming an awkward mood killer. Whatever romance was brewing, gone, with each pain taking effort. Finally, after what seemed an eternity, it went on, but the experience lost. I don't believe it was her first time, especially when she starting helping me with my inexperience.

Over time, things tended to get more comfortable. Although my sexual prowess was average, I suspect my moves with the ladies began to improve, and I no longer felt the uncomfortable situations of my youth. The one at home is the fourth or fifth and only one for some six-years until that unforgettable night. The one that would cost me dearly. The one I could never take back.

And the hotel I dreaded has now become the place I will never forget. Perhaps she knows how I feel, perhaps she doesn't care, yet I will take my cue from her. Somehow or another I'm actually feeling good about this sordid predicament I've put myself in. I'm in one piece, and I feel an inner strength like I've accomplished something worthwhile. When in reality, I know that guilt will creep in my mind as soon as I become fully awake.

It's hard to feel anything but ecstasy when I see her nude body walking to retrieve the newspaper that someone slid under the door sometime this morning. I'm wondering with a sense of pride if he or she heard or could sense what was transpiring on the other side of the door as they laid the newspaper down. Maybe he or she ran and told the whole staff of the going on in room 320. Of the not too subtle pleasurable moaning and groaning. Then when I check out, the entire staff would greet me with a standing ovation. Thumbs up by the men, and jeers from the women. And the desk clerk asking me with a blink of the eye, "how was your stay?"

The sad truth is that we sat like civilized people eating a hearty breakfast and reading the newspaper like any other couple out on holiday. Just two ordinary people who by chance happened to fall in the same bed and for a brief time felt the warmth that each secretly longed for, an unexpected night, lost of any problems or worries about the real-life each lead. Just a couple enjoying warm rolls with marmalade.

We each got dressed with little or no conversation. There wasn't any talk about who was to pick up the kids or what we were having for dinner, and nothing about paying the bills, or who called, nothing remotely connected with the home front. And in some small and twisted way, I didn't miss anything of those things. I wish I had more guilt.

We kissed for a long time and suddenly I felt something that was missing all night long: passion. A strong sense of caring suddenly and without provocation overwhelmed my body and soul. I looked at her beautiful body, not in a lustful way but in a way that didn't want her to leave. I wanted to walk downtown and window shop, stopping to have lunch and dinner and then another night in room #320. Not another shameless filled night, but a more desirable night, bursting with emotion. I wanted to hold and touch her. I needed her!

Suddenly, I found myself asking for her telephone number but more importantly I wanted to know her name and I quickly forgot about the one at home.

So, for the next five months, I continued to see her. We had drinks after work at the Janitor's Closet, a quaint bar at the mall, or she would make sandwiches that we ate at the park, or listen to jazz at the various clubs around town where we could listen to music and dance.

We had gotten beyond the sex, although it continued to be an essential part of the sordid relationship. More importantly, we were becoming good friends. Anytime we were together, I couldn't resist touching her soft skin, and looking at the twinkle in her eyes. She became someone I could confide in and express the frustrations that always centered on a job. A job I no longer care about.

She became the person I trusted the most and had replaced the one at home, especially when I needed to vent. I did my usual amount of complaining, and she listens intently, yet not passing judgment, except to say, "I'm sorry you had a bad day." All my problems solved with just a few words.

I discovered myself getting out of bed and out of the house so I could spend a few hours at her apartment, where she always greeted me wearing a soft yellow negligee. A quickie before I went to the office where nothing exciting happened, and I found myself staring at my watch, ready to leave five minutes after I arrived.

I found myself unraveling. I was trying to keep my stories, or should I say lies, straight and I began making mistakes. Small slip-ups to the eventual blunders and the consideration crossing my mind that perhaps, I wanted to be discovered.

My secret remained just that, but nothing is safe and guarded forever. One day, I became overrun with guilt, which forced me to confess to the one at home. Then without mercy, I found myself living in an efficiency apartment. There wasn't a big fight, just a quick divorce.

My apologies went unheard, even my remorseful plea for another chance went out the window along with my clothes. My amassed small fortune was cut in half, just like my heart. Whatever good attributes I had became a distasteful act of the worse kind of human being. I was pronounced a cheater by our so-call friends who quickly took sides, and I was left alone, not even a chance to talk with their husbands, lest they would meet with the same fate. I had to find another world, another set of friends. I became a leper, a despicable human being.

After my downfall, I lost myself in a world of self-pity. How could this happen to me? Why wouldn't she, the now ex, be more understanding and give me another chance? Questions that I asked myself over and over while I cried in my beer.

For a short time, I quit seeing the other woman, blaming her for my transgression and subsequent downfall. She couldn't quite understand why it was all her fault, and she would call me from time to time just to see if I had hanged or blown my brains out—which I must confess, I considered both options on more than one occasion.

That is until one night, when I was full of anger, self-pity, and had one too many drinks at Chez Nous. I went out in the alley, broke a bottle of beer, and ran it across my wrist. Incredibly, all that you think about is where you wind up and that it has to better than this place.

Unfortunately, I missed the central vein, and found myself standing in a smelly, and dingy ally, looking at my wrist slowly being emptied of blood. In an instant of panic, I tried wrapping my tie around the cut on my wrist, but it wasn't helping. The blood continued to flow. I didn't feel anything. I mean I didn't think about family or friends. Nothing but a sense of relief. I sat in the alleyway with all the vermin, waiting for the end. It was a wait and see, more anticipation than fear. Just waiting.

There's always a do-gooder lurking in every corner, and sure enough, I had my own guardian angel. Not your typical looking angel, with white robe and wings, but a rundown hobo, looking worn around the gills from too many bottles of cheap wine and cigarettes that stained his fingers, and who on most days couldn't find his way in a bathroom. But here he was coming to my aid. He saw my misery and took me to the hospital, where I got scornful looks from doctors and nurses alike. Obligated to patch my wrist, although I'm sure they would have preferred to work on the more deserving ones. I cursed my new-found savior and gave him twenty bucks for saving my worthless life.

I was now a statistic, one of many who attempted and survived the cowardly deed, that could have landed me in the looney ward along with all the people that I had a contempt for earlier in my life. But now, like them, I would forever be branded with a scar of shame.

My survival did nothing for my self-esteem. I continued working, although now I felt alienated from those who were and should've been my closest allies. I walked around like a zombie. And even on some of my loneliest nights, I found myself driving through my old neighborhood, for one last glimpse of the house where I had experienced so many good times…more self-torture!

The passage of time cures all, and I found myself taking a new job in another state. The misery of the past is gone with everything I dumped in the trash bin before I left.

And I saw the one who guided me down the path of destruction, and love. She was getting married, and she looked happy. Although I saw a glimpse in her eyes that said, "take me with you," but alas it couldn't be. So I kissed her cheek, and said goodbye. Each of us with tears in our eyes.

As much as I wanted her, I couldn't because I was beginning to like my single life such as it was. But clearly, I would miss her and never regretted the first of our many nights together.

What could have been, had I been more in touch with my feelings that perhaps I could express them more freely, instead of bottling up the emotions that would haunt me time and again.

Before I left town, I also drove to my ex's house to say goodbye. She was outside working in the garden with her new man. We exchanged pleasantries, and she wished me well, and somehow, I felt a deep profound. My heart-ached, and I wished I could have said more than, "see you."

It would be many years before, I saw her again.

I can't explain the sad, tragic feeling as I packed all my belongings into my car and then driving off, leaving behind the place where I was born and reared to know that I would never return.

I thought about my parents, who sadly hugged me and then waved goodbye as I drove off. Memories I will miss forever. How did they know that their middle son would move away from home and become a ghost they only saw occasionally over the years?

Almost as important, I would have to leave friends who I grew up with and had my first drinks with, and my first intimate conversations, and the bread we broke over and over again. Close friends that I will never see again, no matter how hard I will try.

On my last night, the gang gave me a going-away party. Everyone I knew was there, including Roberta, who was my latest companion. I had a rather unusual relationship with Roberta. I never asked where she lived or asked for her telephone number or anything else that might make our relationship loving. If we had a date, my friend Doug would pick her up at her house and when Roberta and I were finished whatever we were doing, Doug would take her home. I wanted her company but nothing else.

The night of the party was no exception. I held her tight while we danced, I could tell that she was getting teary-eyed. This wouldn't be a sad goodbye. The only person missing from the party was my best friend, John. But as was his custom, he showed up late, carrying a fifth of Johnny Walker Black. We made our exit from the party and spent the rest of the evening in the park talking about all the good times we had in the past and drinking Johnny Walker Black. John was the only person who stuck with me after the divorce.

Early the next morning, I said my goodbye to John, and we swore that we would keep in touch. That was the last time I saw John, Doug, and Roberta.

Years later, Roberta found me and called, and she asked if she could come and live with me. As much as I wanted to say yes, I instead said no. Nonetheless, I did care about her, but she never knew. This would be the first of many relationships where I would just walk away.

My only thought for leaving was to get away from all the sorrow that I caused myself and others. But now I see another side, a chance to start again.

As I packed the final box into my car, I felt sad, and I wished there was something I could do, like back out of this new job. I wanted to stay and fight it out and to be a better person, but alas, that just wasn't going to work. I had to go!

I suppose, I wondered what it would be like to live in another city or state, but I never thought it would come to fruition. But as I drove down the freeway, I feel exhilaration, a calmness, internal strife, a new-found sense of energy, like the first time I rode my bicycle down the mountain. Dangerous, exciting, and scared but wondering why I hadn't done it before.

My drive from start to finish is approximately twelve hours. This, of course, is my furthest road trip, so, I had to remember to stop, gas up, and use the facilities, lest I will find myself stranded in the desert, for merely looking at the beautiful vistas instead of paying attention to my car's needs.

Stucky's Truck Stop ahead. I've never been to a Stucky's before, but I instantly feel like a kid. I pull to the gas pump, and the attendant begins to fill the car, then he washes the windshield, and checks the oil. I pull forward and enter Stucky's, which is a combination restaurant and curio shop. I sit at the counter and look at the menu that is handed to me by a waitress, with her red hair stacked like a beehive, and dressed in a white dress, wearing a name tag that proudly announces her name as Maggie.

Maggie seems distant and distracted, perhaps it has to do with the loudness of the place. Who knows, and who really cares because all I want was service. I ordered a cold roast beef sandwich and a coke. For some unknown reason, the lunch was delicious. It must be Stuckey's unique cooking process or better yet, I was just hungry, and that probably even eating the soles of my shoes would've tasted good. After eating, I browsed through the shop and couldn't believe all the items they stock. It's unreal, everything from rubber snakes to maps, which is my primary interest at the time. Somehow buying the map made it official. I'm off to live in another state.

It's dusk, and the sun is setting quietly in the east. The last sign I passed indicates ten miles to my new home. Off in the distance, I can see a glimmer of lights, and without notice, the traffic is increasing. Five miles and street sign exits are becoming more prominent. Central Ave exists in two miles. This is where I get off, I can see a few motels. This is where I will spend my first of several nights. As it turns out, Central Avenue is the main thoroughfare of my new home.

I check-in, take the key from the clerk, and make my way to room 101. I hang my clothes and make myself comfortable in bed, suddenly there is a knock at the door. I get up, answer the door, and there is a young Hispanic woman handing me towels. I take the bath towels, and we begin to talk, primarily about where I from and the such. Short story, we found each other in bed. Welcome to my new home.

I tackled my new job as a prisoner on parole. My introverted personality began to change, I was now able to extravert when I wanted, and of course, when it was a benefit to me. I began to take more control of my life again. My only responsibility was to me, and that's all that mattered. My sorrowful past, slowly drifting away with each passing day.

Gradually, I began to forget about that first night and the subsequent months that followed. Yet, for the first time in my life, I admitted secretly that I loved that woman, but I squandered that opportunity because I was me.

My first acquaintance in my new home was Fred. Fred knew everyone in the city, and everyone knew Fred. The fantastic thing about Fred was that he never bought a drink at any bar he went to because somebody was always sending bottles to the table...lots of drinks.

My first weekend in town, Fred invited me to his house for breakfast. His wife was out of town visiting her mother for the weekend, and Fred was playing bachelor. He scrambled some eggs, added green Chile, then plated it with refried beans and warm tortillas. It was just like being at home. After the feast, Fred drove me around town, primarily to show me all the best bars, best Mexican food restaurants, and what areas to stay clear. After a day of sightseeing, he took me to Michael's to shoot pool and drink beer. That was my beginning, and within three months, I knew everyone Fred knew. I was like the new kid in school, I was a hit.

I met all the other gang members, yet it was Fred and Joe who were my running around buddies. There wasn't a single night that didn't find us at either Michael's or La Anita, drinking red beer and shooting pool. I was the only single guy in the group, yet somehow or another, all of the gang were out every night. We thought we were really cool guys and even had our own terminology. For example, we called women snakes, the bars we frequented were snake pits, and we were snake killers. How about that for being clever?

There were six of us who traveled to the same towns, and from the time we arrived on Monday to the time we left on Thursdays, it was non-stop drinking, chasing women, and working. Whatever we did or were, we worked hard and partied even harder. We were good at our craft, and we knew it.

I was beginning to excel beyond anything that my buddies could imagine. As the year worn on, I began to disassociate myself from the guys who didn't share the same ambition that I had. I was going through another transformation.

It was during my period of alteration that I met a man who was much older than me. His name was Ivan. Ivan was a man who everyone respected for being good at his job and for just being a good man. Ivan had a kind word to everyone. Ivan and I would meet at a downtown coffee shop and talk about business, about world events, and his family that he was proud of. I learned a great deal during my meetings with Ivan. He was a great guy who died a year after I met him.

I was learning my craft, my new vocation; I was a damn good salesman. I enrolled at the local university and took business and marketing classes. I made mental notes of all the sales techniques. I quickly discounted the bad ones but started to incorporate the good stuff along with my analytic style. I was good, and everyone around me knew it.

It was having lunch or drinks with the most influential people in the food industry, plus, I also met local politicians and even dated a judge.

I was in her courtroom for speeding and running a red light. I, with an effervescent smile, pleaded guilty and threw myself on the mercy of the court. She took one look and with no uncertainty threw my case out the window for lack of evidence or perhaps because I was good looking and full of BS. Of course, our tryst only lasted one night, and that was fine with me, but I became more cautious about my drinking and driving.

When it came to romantic relationships, I took the process of meeting someone thoughtfully. I wasn't in for casual encounters, but unfortunately, things never materialized as I planned. I suppose the term "air-head," took a new meaning and seldom did anyone last more than two weeks.

There were a few that made the cut, but I quickly became bored. I found myself comparing everyone to the one I really loved back home who was to marry another, and that became problematic as time went on. I continued to carry a torch, so when it came to affairs of the heart, I took a huge step backward. I was better with casual one-night stands that offered nothing but sex.

It was about this time that I needed a change. So, I took up abstract oil painting, and for a while I felt like Picasso, generating artwork that made absolutely no sense to anyone. Except for the vivid colors, they appeared to be painted by a five-year-old. So I went back to women.

On one of my nights out, I met a young Asian man, whose name escapes me. We talked well into the night about Taoism. He seemed at peace with everything and was understanding of my boundless inquiries. I met with him several times after our initial meeting, and the more he talked about Taoism, the more I became convinced that this is what I needed in my life.

I began the study of Tao, one book after the other, and rather than have a better understanding, I became confused. I didn't comprehend, it wasn't making any sense. It was leaving me with one unanswered question after the other. With considerable frustration, I sought my Asian friend. I need clarification. However, he had moved on, so I had to find the answers on my own.

In retrospect, I was looking for something tangible, like in the teachings of Christianity. What I found was that Tao, for me, stood for something much higher and more significant but that didn't have a deity. I found a more philosophical balance with nature and the spirit world. A clear understanding and acceptance of the differences that exist.

However, my most significant change happened after studying the I Ching. It helped me appreciate and to work with the diverse changes, so subtle, that are always transpiring. It helped to understand the hidden powers at work in my unconscious spiritual being that is working behind the scenes, the process of self-realization, and my continual process of transformation. Of course, there was much more, but I became a student for over thirty years.

Not only did Taoism change my life forever, but my outlook on human nature. Even accelerating a need to help others, which went totally against my temperament in past years. The years where I cared for no one, also going out of my way to be unkind, especially to women.

I even became monogamous for the first time in years. A relationship was so rare that every day became a joyful experience. My only hunger was to be with her, doing everything together, yet doing nothing. It didn't matter as long as we were together. But it was to last for only a year before she was killed, and I went to hell once again.

Not even my Taoism could help me. I suddenly became the person I despised the most. I now found myself associating with the lowest, sleaziest, most despicable people imaginable. The druggies and whores who brought me no comfort except for the night. Going to the places where I was advised not to enter.

Once I found myself waking up with men and woman on a single mattress. Broken glass and dented cans, drugs of every type scattered through the floor. And a vile stench that permeated throughout this den of disillusionment. I got up and made my way out, the sunlight blinding my eyes as I opened the door. Then realizing that I didn't know where I was or how I got there.

And once even waking up in the back seat of a car that was parked on a mountain road. The humiliation it brought lasted only a few hours, then I was in search of where to score my next joint, or where I could get a drink to calm my nerves.

The self-respected human that I was a few months before was now crawling out of bed, barely able to work without some drug to wake my body. My desire to be the best was instantly gone in a cloud of booze or whatever. My friends began to disassociate themselves from me, the leper.

One morning, as I stood in front of the mirror shaving, I noticed someone sitting at the foot of my bed. Startled, I turned around and saw a vision of my lost love. The one who I mourned for days and nights. She said that she was alright and that it was time for me to move on. I sat on the bed and cried, not for myself but for her, and asked for forgivingness.

That was my new beginning. I cleaned up. I quit hanging with the degenerates and went back to work. I was on a mission again. But first, I had to apologize to my friends who I had abandoned.

A couple of weeks later, I received a call from my paramour. We hadn't talked in years, yet we started our conversation as thou we had chatted just yesterday. We talked about our respective lives and her kids, and even about her husband. We talked about her vacations… on and on.

Then out of nowhere I broke down and told that I had loved her for all these years. There was a silence and I began to think that perhaps I had overstepped my boundaries. "You took my breath away," she said. It sounded like a good thing, then I proceeded to cleanse my soul and started to recount all my affairs and indiscretions, a confession, reminiscent of my boyhood days when I went to the confessional booth weekly. She listened to me without condemnation, just words of encouragement.

I promised to go and see her and to meet her family and she agreed. It would, however, take months before I had enough courage and go, but a promise is a promise.

She picked me at the airport, and we drove to the hotel where I would stay. A journey in total silence. I felt uncomfortable, and I began to regret beginning there. When we arrived, I got out and took my bags, and unsure of what to say, I just stood. She got out of the car, walked in my direction, and instantly fell into my arms. Just holding her would have been enough, but there we were in room 120, overlooking the pool, in bed like we had so many years past.

What can I tell you? Our one-night stand lasted for thirty-years. We continued to see other as our time permitted, and it was always like the first time. Our comfort with each other was undeniable, and we had love without question.

When I went to visit, we made it a point of doing something different each time. We went on walks through historic neighborhoods, we went window shopping at the mall, we ate lunch at various restaurants, and one afternoon took in a matinee. A great couple we made.

Of course, no one knew except her oldest daughter, who surprisingly supported her mother because she knew that she was being loved in a way that no one else could love her.

Over time, our conversations drifted from her grown children to her grandchildren. I was involved in her life, and she was mine. My love for her grew daily.

I never had a family of my own, so I lived vicariously through all the family drama, the colds, the doctor visits, sometimes offering consoling advise when she became too stressed out with her daily life. I was invited to be part of the family and I took full advantage, even though I lived hundreds of miles away.

Years later, I begged her to leave her husband, but she declined my offer. She didn't want to leave her family. I understood, and so I never asked again. Not many people get a second chance in life; I was given my second chance, and I wasn't going to screw it up like I had the first time.

My second chance also taught me something, and that is to say what and how I feel. So every time we talk, I never fail to say, "I love you." But more importantly, I've learned that it's not wrong to want something that you will never get.

About the Author

The suffering that comes from being an abused child transmits a shame that encompasses every aspect of one's life. Hidden guilt that changes who you are to someone else; your virtue taken in one single moment. There was a time when putting together a legible sentence was unfathomable. So, in desperation to suppress the social ineptness, writing became an escape.

The selections in *Too Poor to Afford a Pencil* originated from heartfelt stories I heard while traveling across the country. How much truth in each? I can only speculate. A few, of course, are personal narratives. A page-turner, the book does not have to be read chronologically.

Samuel Ramos was born and reared in Miami, Arizona. He graduated from Miami High School, studied at St. Louis University and Creative Writing at Wesleyan University and is a retired food executive. His first book entitled *The Appointment* recounts the murder of three Mexican miners in Globe, Arizona, circa 1908. A highly respected police officer, Marshall Pena, was dispatched to Globe to solve the crime.

CPSIA information can be obtained
at www.ICGtesting.com
Printed in the USA
LVHW030929210221
679521LV00004B/482